W9-CCA-610

WATCH HOLLOW

GREGORY FUNARO

WATCH HOLLOW

HARPER
An Imprint of HarperCollinsPublishers

Library of Congress Control Number: 2018952012

ISBN 978-0-06-264345-2 (trade bdg.)

Typography by Chelsea C. Donaldson

18 19 20 21 22 CG/LSCH 10 9 8 7 6 5 4 3 2 1

❖

First Edition

218 1174

For Abby.

And, as always, for my daughter.

"The oldest and strongest emotion of mankind is fear, and the oldest and strongest kind of fear is fear of the unknown."

—H. P. Lovecraft

PROLOGUE

The rat, Fennish Seven, pumped his legs harder toward the river. He could see a circle of moonlight now at the edge of the woods—about thirty yards ahead, at the end of the tunnel of trees. But the Garr was gaining fast.

"*I WANT YOUR FEAR, FENNISH SEVEN!*" he bellowed.

The earth shook with the giant's footsteps—*boom, boom, boom!*—and then came the thunderous crack of splitting tree limbs.

Startled, Fennish stumbled and nearly fell, then quickly found his footing again and took off down the leaf-strewn path. He didn't dare look back—the rat was so frightened, he could hardly breathe.

"*THERE IS NO ESCAPE, SEVEN!*" the giant cried again—closer now, *boom, boom, boom!*—and Fennish turned on a final burst of speed. His heart hammered, and his legs throbbed painfully. Twenty yards—*boom!*—ten yards—*boom, boom, boom!*—and then the rat hurled himself out of the woods and into the moonlight. He scrambled down the riverbank and leaped for the water when, without warning, a pair of sharp talons dug into his flesh and snatched him up in the air.

It was the giant's bird—the traitor, Tempus Crow.

"Aaaagggghhh!" cried Fennish, struggling against the crow's grasp; and then the Garr's laughter, deep and croaking, echoed through the woods.

"YOU ARE MINE, SEVEN!"

Fennish Seven twisted and thrashed as Tempus Crow carried him higher, and then, somehow, the rat craned his head back over his shoulder and sank his teeth into the underside of the great bird's thigh. It was the old wound, still tender from the first time they'd fought, and with an ear-splitting *"Caw!"* the traitor released him.

Fennish tumbled head over tail through the darkness; but just before he splashed down in the river, he caught sight of the Garr's red, burning eyes glaring hatefully at him through the trees.

After that, everything went black.

ONE

MR. QUIGLEY'S PROPOSAL

The long black car brought the rain. Or was it the other way around? Lucy Tinker could never be sure, but in the end, it didn't matter. There was darkness in both.

Lucy watched the car from her father's storefront window, her eyes peering out through the backward *O* and *C* in *CLOCK* as if the painted letters were spectacles. The car had been sitting there for about fifteen minutes. So had Lucy, cross-legged, in a spot once occupied by a large mantel clock her father had sold the day before.

If any strangers had been passing by Tinker's Clock Shop that day, they might have thought Lucy were for sale, too, wedged as she was among the other objects in the window. There were clocks, of course, but also two Chinese vases, a painting of a poodle in a tutu, and a rusty old tuba.

"No, Pop, you need to move the decimal point over *two* spaces," Oliver said. He was helping their father balance the books on the ancient laptop behind the counter—and from the sound of things, Pop wasn't happy.

"You mean we lost six *hundred* and forty dollars? Not six dollars and forty cents?"

"And I haven't even factored in the interest on the line of credit yet."

Mr. Tinker groaned and held his head in his hands. "I knew I shouldn't have bought that tuba!"

Oliver met Lucy's eyes and shrugged. He'd warned Pop not to branch out into antiques. But Pop hadn't listened, and it had cost him big-time. Lucy wasn't sure how much, only that, over the last year, there had been less money to spend on groceries each week.

Lucy sighed and swiveled her eyes up to an old cuckoo clock on the wall. Only three minutes left until closing. Three little ticks on the big hand and then *cuckoo!*—her punishment was over. That's what you got for fighting these days: *five days* of hard labor in the clock shop. Didn't matter that the fight was on the last day of school, or that Betty Bigsby had it coming. Pop wouldn't listen. Pop *never* listened.

Lucy *hated* being cooped up in her father's shop. It was smaller than the other stores on their dingy city street and smelled like an old shoe, not to mention the constant chorus of ticking drove her bonkers. But that's the way life was sometimes, right? You had to roll with the punches. And when Betty Bigsby yanked her braid and called her a food stamp freak . . . well, Lucy was pretty good at rolling out some punches of her own.

Lucy's eyes drifted back to the car outside. The rain had changed direction, and she could now make out the shadow of a man in the driver's seat.

"What are you waiting for, superstar?" Lucy muttered

as she twirled her single braid of black hair between her fingers. Yeah, whoever this guy was, he had to be rich with a set of wheels like that. Maybe if he bought something, Pop would forget about how bad business was. At least for a little while.

"Why don't you close up, Ollie?" he said, still hunched over the computer, and Oliver ducked out from beneath the counter.

"Hold up a sec," Lucy said, and she jerked her chin at the car. "I think this dude's waiting for the rain to die down."

Oliver pushed his glasses higher on his nose and peered out from behind the shop's Open sign. "He's not coming in here," he said. "Probably just lost or something."

"How much you want to bet?"

"Loser does the laundry solo tomorrow."

The children shook hands on it, and in the next moment, the clocks in the shop began to chime. At the same time, a big black umbrella blossomed out from the car and began heading straight for the door. Lucy smiled smugly.

"Have fun," she said, holding up a peace sign, and Oliver sighed and joined their father again behind the counter. The customer bell dinged, and a small, somewhat round, elderly gentleman dressed in black entered the store.

"Mr. Tinker, I presume?" he said, removing his hat. The old man appeared to be bald except for a pair of white tufts

8

above his ears, but it was hard to tell because he wore a bandage on his head. Beneath his large nose was a bushy white mustache, and he sounded British, Lucy thought—like one of those rich snots from Weston.

"Er—yes, that's me," Mr. Tinker said, fingering his collar.

"Ah, the legend himself!" the old man said, and he hung up his hat and umbrella on the coat rack. "Forgive me for calling on you so late in the day, Mr. Tinker, but I'd hoped to avoid an unwanted shower."

The old man chuckled and coughed into a handkerchief.

"How can I help you, Mr.—?"

"Quigley," he said, straightening the bandage on his head. "Mortimer Quigley. And you are Charles Tinker, clocksmith extraordinaire." Mr. Tinker just stared back at the old man blankly. "You *are* the same Charles Tinker who repaired the city clock tower after the infamous lightning strike ten years ago, aren't you?"

"Oh *that*! Yes—that's me. But it was hardly anything—er—legendary."

"Don't be modest," said Mr. Quigley, wagging his finger. "The way I hear it, all the king's horses and all the king's men couldn't put that clock together again—that is, until Charles Tinker came along."

Mr. Tinker blushed. "Well, that's a bit of an exaggeration, but—"

"And who's that hiding there behind you?" asked Mr. Quigley, his eyes landing on Oliver.

"Er—this is my son, Oliver. He just turned thirteen. And over there in the window is my daughter, Lucy. She's eleven."

"Don't tell me you're planning on selling her along with that tuba?"

Mr. Quigley chuckled and coughed again into his handkerchief.

"That might not be a bad idea," Mr. Tinker said flatly, and Lucy pursed her lips. She knew her father was joking, but his words stung just the same. Oliver was his favorite. They were a lot alike, father and son—tall, skinny, red-headed, and both whizzes when it came to fixing things. Lucy, on the other hand, could hardly fix a sandwich, and looked nothing like her father. She was short for her age, with long raven hair that she always wore in a braid just like her mother used to.

Her mother . . .

Lucy's heart twisted. She missed her mom more than she could stand sometimes. It had been two years since the cancer took her, but the missing still always hit Lucy as it did now—sudden and heavy in her chest, like the torrential rain that had descended on the city just as the long black car arrived.

Mr. Quigley regarded Lucy sympathetically, as if he were reading her mind.

"Well, thank goodness at least *one* thing in that window is priceless," the old man said with a wink, and Lucy felt the corners of her lips turn up in a smile.

"What can I do for you, Mr. Quigley?"

"Charles Tinker, I have a business proposal for you." Mr. Quigley slipped a small velvet pouch out from under his coat and plopped it on the counter with a *clink*. "Before we address the details, however, might I suggest we speak in private?"

Mr. Tinker's eyes darted awkwardly between his children. "Oliver is my right-hand man. Anything you can say to me you can say to him. And Lucy there—well—"

"Say no more, Warden," she said, hopping down. "So, I'm officially on parole?"

Mr. Tinker smiled thinly. "You'll have to excuse my daughter, Mr. Quigley. She's been grounded all week. Fighting at school. Not the first time."

Lucy's cheeks grew hot. True, it *wasn't* the first time—and not the second or third time either—but it wasn't as if Betty and those other clowns didn't deserve it. And why did Pop have to go and tell Mr. Quigley?

"I understand," said Mr. Quigley, and his face grew serious. "It's none of my business, but I too lost someone very

11

dear to me at a young age. Children deal with grief differently, Mr. Tinker, but I've always believed that, in the end, all they really need is someone to listen."

An uncomfortable silence hung about the shop, and yet Lucy swore the ticking of the clocks grew louder. The Tinkers didn't know what to say.

"How did you know?" Mr. Tinker asked finally, and Mr. Quigley nodded at the picture of Lucy's mother hanging behind the counter—her old headshot from when she was with the Boston Ballet. Eyes confident and yet vulnerable, the corners of her mouth turned up in a knowing smile— just like the Mona Lisa, Lucy's father always said.

"I do not enter into business arrangements without doing my homework," said Mr. Quigley. "And so, allow me to express my condolences on the loss of your wife."

"Yes—er—thank you," said Mr. Tinker, shifting uneasily on his feet. "Lucy, why don't you throw that leftover pizza into the microwave. This shouldn't take too long."

Lucy nodded and walked in a daze toward the family's tiny, one-room apartment at the back of the shop. She'd been counting the minutes to this moment all day, but now . . . what a strange guy this Mr. Quigley was! And before she realized what she was doing, Lucy hid under her father's worktable and listened.

"Very well, then," said Mr. Quigley. "I come to you in

12

desperate need of your services at Blackford House."

"I'm sorry—Blackford House?"

"The name of my new home. It is located in Watch Hollow, Rhode Island, and was originally constructed with a magnificent clock in one of its walls. I acquired the house a few months ago, you see, and am in the process of renovating it before relocating permanently to the States from my native England."

Lucy peeked out from behind the worktable. Her father and Mr. Quigley were still by the cash register, but Oliver had drifted away somewhat and was staring straight at her from behind the counter. The idiot—he was going to blow her cover. Lucy motioned for him to turn back to the adults, and with a roll of his eyes, Oliver did.

"Surely you didn't have to travel all the way up from Rhode Island to find someone who could fix this clock of yours, Mr. Quigley."

"Oh, I *did* find someone else, but he could make neither head nor tail of it. You see, the clock in question is no ordinary clock. It generates electricity for the entire house, which is presently without power. Thus, the clock needs to be repaired before I can move in. Only a man of *your* expertise can get the job done in a timely manner—no pun intended." Mr. Quigley chuckled and coughed into his handkerchief. "Even so, I expect the job will take at least a few weeks, which is why my offer is contingent on your residence at Blackford House."

"But Mr. Quigley, I just can't up and leave my children. I'm all they have."

"You misunderstand me. Your children are to come with you. There are adequate servants' quarters located in the rear of the house, and all your needs shall be provided for. The only stipulation is that you get the job done, no questions asked. And, of course, you shall be compensated handsomely for your . . . *discretion*."

Mr. Quigley dumped out what looked like a dozen or so gold coins from the velvet pouch onto the counter.

"I—er—" Mr. Tinker stammered. "Forgive me, Mr. Quigley, but where I come from, if something sounds too good to be true, it usually is."

"I assure you, both my offer and these coins are genuine." Mr. Quigley fished out a business card from his pocket and slid it across the counter. "A quick Google search should suffice as a background check. However, should you care to speak to someone personally about my reputation, I've listed the phone numbers for some of my associates in London on the back of my card. Just remember the five-hour time difference."

Mr. Quigley chuckled and gave another cough into his handkerchief, and as her father examined the business card, Lucy realized that her heart was pounding. Pop was right—the whole thing sounded too good to be true.

"Those coins are only a tenth of what I intend to pay you for your services," said Mr. Quigley, adjusting his bandage, and Mr. Tinker's jaw nearly hit the floor. Oliver's, too. "Do not look so shocked, Mr. Tinker. Your luck has finally taken a turn for the better. And if you'll forgive the *intended* pun, I'd say it's *about time*."

Mr. Quigley chuckled and began coughing violently into his handkerchief. Oliver handed him a bottle of Poland Spring from the fridge under the counter, and the old man gulped the water down greedily.

"Thank you, lad," he said, wiping his mouth. Mr. Quigley set down the bottle and moved to the coatrack. "Consider the gold there an advance on your salary. And should you accept my offer, your services are to commence the day after tomorrow."

Mr. Tinker fingered his collar nervously. "But—that's hardly enough time to—"

"Indeed, time is of the essence," the old man interrupted, carefully squeezing his hat onto his bandaged head. "My affairs in London require my presence there within the week. However, if this is too much of an inconvenience, perhaps you might refer me to someone else?"

"No, no," Mr. Tinker said quickly. "It's just that—well—I'll have to check these out." He nodded at the coins, and Mr. Quigley smiled and grabbed his umbrella.

"But of course," he said, heading for the door. Mr. Tinker followed him. "You can reach me with your decision at the number on my card. Say, by noon tomorrow?" Mr. Tinker nodded, and Mr. Quigley tipped his hat. "Good afternoon, then."

Mr. Quigley left, dinging the customer bell, and the constant chorus of ticking once again grew louder in Lucy's head. Was Pop really going to drag them down to Rhode Island? Both the swim club and karate camp at the Y started on Monday. And what about her summer soccer league at the park? Lucy was their best goalie!

"Pop, there are ten of these," Oliver said—he'd moved over to the coins while Lucy was daydreaming. "They're one ounce each. Meaning, if these are real—"

"I know." Mr. Tinker flipped the Open sign to Closed and locked the door.

"Last I checked, the price of gold was twelve hundred bucks per *ounce!*" Oliver's voice cracked shrilly on "ounce."

Math wasn't Lucy's strong suit, but even she knew that ten times twelve hundred was twelve *thousand*. And if what Mr. Quigley said was true, twelve thousand was one tenth of—

"One hundred and twenty thousand *doll*-ars!" Oliver

cried, his voice cracking again. "We can pay off the line of credit and still have plenty left over!"

Oliver whirled and began furiously tapping away on the laptop, while Mr. Tinker scooped up the coins and brought them over to the worktable. He was so preoccupied, he didn't even notice Lucy as she stepped aside to make room for him.

"Pop," Lucy began, but her father raised his hand to shush her. He sat down at the worktable and removed a small vial of liquid from the drawer. Then he made a tiny scratch on the edge of one of the coins and, using the vial's dropper, applied a small drop of the liquid to the scratch.

"No reaction to the nitric acid," he said. "This one looks legit."

Lucy watched in numb fascination as her father tested each coin, and by the time he had finished, his hands were visibly shaking with excitement. All the coins were real. Twelve thousand dollars in *real gold* sitting right there on his worktable. Lucy had never seen so much money in her life. Neither had her father, from the looks of him.

"One hundred and twenty thousand dollars," he muttered to himself. "Just for fixing some dumb clock down in Rhode Island."

Unbelievable, Lucy thought. Her father could finally afford that new truck and the MacBook he'd been wanting for the business—not to mention the iPads he'd been promising her and Oliver for years now, too. He might even throw them each a new iPhone if they played their cards right. The rich girls at school always had the latest one. Food stamp freak my fanny!

"Looks like this Mortimer Quigley is some kind of wealthy philanthropist," Oliver called from the computer. "I can't find anything about Blackford House, but Google shows Watch Hollow being out in the boonies near Conn-ect-ticut."

Lucy bit her lip and stifled a giggle. Oliver's voice had been cracking a lot lately—just puberty, Pop had explained—but Lucy suspected the pimples on his chin and forehead had more to do with stress. Oliver had taken their mother's death harder than anyone—so much so that he had to stay back in fifth grade. And on the rare occasions when he wasn't working in the shop, his nose was buried in his stupid comic books. He hardly ever hung out with his friends anymore. True, most of them were in middle school now, but still . . .

"So, what do you think, Pop?" Oliver said, hurrying over, and Mr. Tinker slipped the pouch of gold into a steel box that was hidden beneath the floorboards under his worktable.

"I think things are finally looking up for the Tinkers,"

he said, and Lucy saw that her father's eyes were misty with tears.

Impulsively, Lucy threw her arms around his waist, and he hugged her back—awkwardly at first, but then tighter as Oliver joined in. And the three of them just stood there like that, hugging one another for the first time since Mom's funeral.

Only this hug was different, Lucy thought; and definitely worth way more than a hundred and twenty thousand dollars.

TWO

BAGS AND BIGSBYS

The next morning, Oliver sat at the kitchen table, pushing his spoon absently at his cereal as he watched his father comb his hair in their tiny bathroom. The mirror had a crack down the middle, so he had to keep bobbing his head side to side to get a good view—like some redheaded hip-hop dancer, Oliver thought.

"I shouldn't be too long, Ollie," his father called through the open door. "The gold dealer is only two blocks away. He'll cut me a check, and then I'll head over to the bank to make my deposit. After that, I'll take care of the overdue payments on the line of credit. With this twelve thousand, we should be clear until December. Boy, won't those bigwig bankers be surprised. No bankruptcy for Tinker's Clock Shop after all!"

Mr. Tinker chuckled and patted the pocket of his hooded sweatshirt, where the pouch of gold had been hidden ever since he'd gotten dressed. Before that, it had been tucked under his pillow. Oliver had heard his father retrieve the pouch from the shop late last night. Must've been so excited that he couldn't sleep a wink.

Oliver figured this was true because his father's snoring usually woke him up at least once during the night. If not that, it was Lucy kicking him in the chest. They slept head to toe in a twin bed on one side of the room, while their father slept on a narrow cot on the other side near the stove. The one-room apartment in which they lived was cramped and dark, with only a small window in the bathroom and a door leading to the alley out back.

When Oliver's mother was alive, the Tinkers lived in the apartment upstairs. But with all the medical bills and business being so bad these last couple of years . . . well, truth be told, it wasn't so much that business was bad, but more that Oliver's father was bad at business. Case in point: he was totally wrong about how long the money from Mr. Quigley would last. Oliver figured through September at the latest, but he didn't say anything. His father wouldn't listen anyway; and besides, Oliver couldn't remember the last time he'd seen him so happy.

Mr. Tinker exited the bathroom and moved to the stove. "Make sure you get Lucy to help you at the Laundromat," he said, pouring some coffee into a travel mug. "She's already at the park, I bet—playing soccer before it gets too hot."

Oliver gave his father a thumbs-up, and Mr. Tinker slipped out the back door humming cheerfully. Oliver just sat there for a moment listening as the tune trailed off down the alley. Even if he hadn't lost his bet with Lucy, Oliver still wouldn't have asked her to help him with the laundry. Let her enjoy her parole, he thought—not to mention she was being a good sport about having to miss out on all the stuff she'd planned for the summer.

Well, maybe not the *whole* summer. Oliver couldn't imagine it would take that long to fix a clock—even a giant clock like the one at Blackford House. What a weird name for a house, Oliver thought. But even weirder was the fact that they'd be living there with no electricity. True, his father was bringing the generator, but it was noisy and even worse on gas than their old pickup truck.

Oliver gulped down the rest of his cereal, washed and dried his bowl, and then shoved the dirty dish towel into one of two overstuffed laundry bags. They had so much stuff to do before their trip, his father had decided to close the shop on a Saturday for the first time since Mom died.

Oliver swiveled his eyes to the picture of her atop the single dresser they all shared. Oliver had taken it himself during a family vacation at the beach in Rhode Island when he was eight—the ocean at her back, her hair like frozen black fire in the wind. That was before the chemo. But even in the end, when her hair was short and she weighed less than he did, Oliver thought Eleanor Tinker was the most beautiful woman he'd ever seen.

Tears welled in his eyes, and Oliver snatched an old, tattered issue of *Batman* from atop the dresser and began to read. All the best superheroes had lost someone they loved when they were kids—Superman and Batman, their parents; Spider-Man, his uncle Ben. Not that Oliver thought he was a superhero, but reading about them sometimes made him feel better when the pain became too much.

Thankfully, this was one of those times; and after a couple of pages, his grief subsided. Oliver tucked the comic under his arm, bear-hugged the laundry bags to his chest, and then squeezed with them out the back door into the alley. The Laundromat was only a half block away, but the bags were so heavy, and the place was so hot, by the time he'd loaded everything into the washer, beads of sweat had broken out on his forehead.

Oliver dragged his wrist across his brow and felt the dull ache of a new pimple forming. Going to be a whopper, he could tell, and his stomach twisted anxiously. Great. The more he stressed, the more pimples he got, and the more pimples he got, the more he stressed. A vicious cycle, his father said—like a perpetual motion clock that went on ticking forever.

Oliver sat down in the breeze from the open door, and over the next hour and a half, read his comic book seven times, pausing once to switch the laundry from the washer into the dryer and then again to fold the clean clothes back into the laundry bags. The Laundromat was oddly deserted for a Saturday, but still, Oliver decided to leave the comic on the table. No doubt there would be some kid coming in later with his mother who hadn't read it yet.

Oliver double-knotted the laundry bag cords, heaved the hefty bundles up into his arms, and stepped outside. The late-morning sun was blinding, which is why he didn't see Betty Bigsby and her Neanderthal brother, Theo, until it was too late.

"Going somewhere, *Stinker*?" Theo said, blocking his way, and Oliver gasped.

Theo Bigsby was the same age as Oliver, but because he'd moved on to middle school last fall with the rest of the kids in Oliver's class, Oliver hadn't seen him all year. In the meantime, Theo Bigsby had gotten . . . well . . . *bigger*. His black hair was gelled up in spikes, and he was dressed in a blue Adidas tracksuit that he wore unzipped over a white wife beater. A thick gold chain hung around his fat neck, and his eyes were slits of anger below his heavy, unibrow-lined forehead.

"Where's your sister?" Theo asked through gritted teeth.

"Waiting in line for food stamps, I bet," Betty said, peeking out from behind him. She was dressed in jean shorts and a sparkly T-shirt that said Epic! But other than that, she looked like a smaller, curly haired version of her Neanderthal brother.

"That so, zit-face?" Theo said. "You Stinkers on food stamps now?"

Oliver swallowed hard. The Bigsbys lived in an old town house six blocks away across the tracks on Broadway—not the richest neighborhood, but rich enough that Theo and Betty thought they were better than kids like the Tinkers. So what the heck were they doing over here on the wrong side of the tracks—and on a Saturday, no less?

"We've been lookin' for your sister all week," Theo said, hiking his pants up over his gut, and Betty pulled out her iPhone and started recording. "She jumped Betty here at school. It ain't fair playin' like that. Which is why they're gonna fight again fair and square, and I'm going to record it for my YouTube channel."

Oliver's stomach twisted. He had seen Lucy's fight with Betty on the last day of school. Betty was the one who started it, calling Lucy a food stamp freak and yanking her braid at recess. But there was no use arguing. Theo was an even bigger tool than his sister—the whole family just a bunch of tools living in one big toolshed.

"You still ain't answered my question, zit-face," Theo said, pushing him. "We got subscribers waiting all week to see this beatdown."

"You know, *The*-o," Oliver said, his voice cracking, "underage fight videos are a violation of YouTube's terms of service." Theo shrugged a *whatever* and fluffed his spikes with his fingers. "Besides," Oliver went on, "Lucy's already paid her dues—been grounded all week. She's in the shop right now helping out my dad."

"Naw, she ain't," Theo said. "We already checked. She ain't at the park neither. So where is she, zits? Or do *you* wanna be the star of my next video?"

Theo pushed Oliver again—*harder*—and Oliver staggered back a step. His heart was hammering now, and his arms were screaming from the weight of the laundry bags. There were some grown-ups milling in and out of the shops, but none of them seemed to notice what was going on. Probably for the best, Oliver figured. Even if someone stuck up for him, Theo would still get in a few good shots before he ran off—not to mention, Oliver would look like a total wuss in Theo's YouTube video.

On the other hand, Oliver thought, maybe he should just stand there and take it. Theo wouldn't post anything if Oliver didn't fight back—he'd look like too much of a bully, and the whole thing would backfire on him. Then again, Theo was slow, Oliver knew—and so was Betty—and even with the laundry bags, he might be able to outrun them back to the shop. It was only about forty yards or so.

All this flashed through Oliver's mind in an instant, but before he could decide what to do, the strangest thing happened.

A shadow swept across Theo's face, and then, out of nowhere, an enormous blob of bird poop splattered half his head.

Oliver and Betty gasped, but it took Theo a couple of seconds to figure out what happened. He wiped off a glob of the poop and smelled it—his mouth hanging open, his unibrow scrunched in confusion as his dull-witted brain struggled to put it together.

"Ew, gross!" Betty screamed, and Theo squinted up at the sky. Oliver, blinded by the sunlight, followed his gaze just long enough to register the hazy, fluttering shape of a bird perched above them atop the lamppost, and then in the next moment, he was dashing down the sidewalk, blinking floaters from his eyes.

"Hey, get back here!" Betty cried.

But Oliver only pumped his legs harder. He was dimly aware of Theo saying, *"Turn that camera off!"* And then Oliver skidded to a stop in front of the shop. His heart seized in terror—the front door's security gate was still locked! There was no way he could make it back inside before the Bigsbys caught up with him!

"You stupid bird!" Theo bellowed, and Oliver whirled. Thankfully, the big tool was still forty yards away in front of the Laundromat, pacing angrily and shaking his fist at the sky. Oliver still couldn't see the bird clearly because

of the sunlight, but Betty was aiming her iPhone at it as if she could.

"I told you to turn that off!" Theo screamed, and in a fit of rage, he snatched his sister's phone and hurled it up at the bird. The throw was way off, and the phone sailed across the street and smashed into a flowerpot on one of the fire escapes. Clumps of dirt rained down onto the sidewalk, a man started yelling, and the Bigsbys took off in the opposite direction. *Oliver's* direction.

"This ain't over, zits!" Theo huffed, his face red and smeared with poop. He tried to push Oliver as he passed, but then Betty crashed into Theo from behind and nearly knocked him over. Theo grumbled some garbled curse words, Betty screamed something about Oliver buying her a new iPhone, and then, mercifully, the Bigsbys disappeared around the corner.

Oliver dropped the laundry bags and collapsed on top of them in a fit of laughter. If only he could post *that* on YouTube!

"Caw!" the bird called, fluttering up off the lamppost and out of sight.

It was a crow, Oliver realized.

The biggest crow he had ever seen.

THREE

INTO THE WOODS

Gazing out from the backseat of her father's pickup, it occurred to Lucy that she had been away from the city precisely three times during her eleven years—twice for vacations up in New Hampshire and once to the beach down in Rhode Island just before her mother got sick. Lucy had only been six, but she remembered the trip as if it were yesterday, including the journey itself.

She remembered an enormous blue bug on the side of the interstate, which she presently found atop the New England Pest Control building while passing through Providence. She also remembered a tall, wooden tower that she and Oliver had climbed. Lucy kept looking for it but after a while gave up, mentioning to Oliver that maybe the tower collapsed or something.

"That tower was near the beach," he said, glancing from his comic book to the combo compass-wristwatch-flashlight he always wore. "Watch Hollow is in western Rhode Island; the beach is east."

Lucy rolled her eyes. Most kids would be using a navigation app on their iPhone or something instead of an old-school compass. But the Tinkers didn't have a lot of things that most families did. Mr. Tinker still used one of those ancient flip phones—not to mention the pickup truck in which they were driving had come off the assembly line long before navigation systems were even invented. *How did people back then survive?* Lucy wondered. After all, her father had nearly swerved off the road twice checking the map on the front seat beside him.

Lucy sighed and trained her eyes out the open window. They had left the interstate about twenty minutes ago, and were out in the boonies somewhere with only woods and the occasional farm flying by. Lucy felt as if they had been driving for days, but it was really only a couple of hours since they'd left home. Still, Lucy didn't think Rhode Island was big enough to have so many boonies, and as the pickup sputtered past yet *another* farm, she began to wonder if her father hadn't gotten them lost.

Lucy felt a lump rise in the back of her throat—it had been coming and going ever since they had left that morning. Sometimes the lump was the excited kind she got when Ian Whitaker borrowed her pencil at school. And at other times, like now, the lump was the sad, achy kind she got when she missed her mother.

Lucy swallowed hard, but the lump didn't go away, so she stuck her head out the window and began counting to see how long she could take the wind in her face. She got all the way up to forty-nine before pulling her head back inside. The lump was gone, but now her ears were ringing, which was why she couldn't hear what her father said as he turned down a dirt road and plunged them deeper into the woods, rattling the electric generator in the truck bed.

After a short distance, Lucy had the sense of first going up and then going down. The pickup clattered over a narrow, stone bridge that spanned a rushing, rocky stream, and then the woods suddenly grew so dark that Lucy's father turned on his headlights. Lucy held her breath—she wasn't sure why—and just when she felt her lungs were about to explode, the trees fell away and she spied a rambling, jagged-roofed house up ahead. It stood at the end of a curved, dirt driveway that was choked with weeds and overgrown in spots with mounds of unkempt shrubbery.

"Say hello to Blackford House," said Mr. Tinker, and Lucy exhaled gratefully.

Once upon a time, when her mother was alive, Pop would take the family on Sunday drives through the nicer neighborhoods, like where Betty Bigsby lived. Even though Lucy hated Betty, she secretly dreamed of living in a real house like hers. Lucy didn't want a mansion—just her own bedroom—but never in a million years did she ever think that dream would come true.

Well, *technically* it still hadn't—the Tinkers were only temporary residents at Blackford House, and would be sleeping in the servants' quarters to boot. But still, Lucy felt the excited lump rise again in her throat. She could at least *pretend* she was rich for a few weeks. And maybe, when the job was done, they would have enough money to move into a house of their own.

Living in Blackford House would be good practice, then, Lucy decided. It was three stories tall, with a covered porch and sharp-peaked gables that jutted out on all sides. Atop the highest of these gables was an odd-looking weathervane, and nestled amid the others, Lucy counted four lofty stone chimneys. On one side of the house, two soaring, multipaned windows reflected the late-morning sun like beaten gold, while the other windows loomed cold and black over the property.

As the truck drew closer, however, Lucy noticed that patches of the house's shingled siding were curled or missing in places, and many of the shutters had fallen off and now stood leaning against the exterior. Lucy thought they looked like gravestones poking up amid the tall grass around the foundation. Creepy, for sure—but the woods, she decided, were the creepiest of all.

Even though it was June, the black, twisted trees were almost entirely bare. And not only did they surround the entire property, they also appeared to be slanting, almost *shrinking* away from the house, as if they were afraid of it.

Lucy gulped, and realized that the lump in her throat

was back—only it wasn't an excited or sad lump anymore; it was a lump of fear.

"Mr. Quigley was supposed to meet us here by now," said Mr. Tinker, and the truck sputtered to a stop in front of the house. The Tinkers got out and stretched, and Lucy noticed the stone steps leading up to the porch were crumbling in places and covered in moss.

"This place is a dump," Oliver said, pushing up his glasses, but his father just ignored him and, opening his phone, heaved a heavy sigh.

"I figured as much," he said, frowning. "Reception is horrible out here, too."

"Of course," Oliver muttered. He stuffed his hands into his jeans pockets and looked around anxiously.

"Great setting for a horror movie, don't you think?" Lucy said—she couldn't resist teasing him. "The mysterious Mr. Quigley invites the unsuspecting Tinker family to stay in his house and then one by one bumps them off to steal their money. Only, the joke is on him. The Tinkers *have* no money."

"Shut up, Lucy," Oliver said, and Lucy giggled. Even though Oliver was two years older, it was really easy to spook him.

"Why don't you kids look around for a bit," said Mr. Tinker. He was moving away from them now, his eyes never leaving his phone as he tried to get better reception. "Just don't wander off. I'll try calling Mr. Quigley to tell him we're here."

Oliver looked apprehensively at Lucy, who promptly grabbed him by the wrist and led him along a weedy, flagstone path around the house. There they found the tall, golden windows that Lucy had seen when they arrived— only now they didn't look golden at all.

"That's because the sun was hitting them at a different angle when we drove up," Oliver remarked. Lucy asked him if they could be solar panels—*Maybe the house had electricity after all,* she thought—but her brother shook his head. The house was too old, he said, and solar panels were always placed on the roof.

"How old do you think this house is?" Lucy asked, and Oliver shrugged.

"At least a hundred years," he said, and turned his eyes toward a large swath of windswept grass that stretched out about thirty yards to the woods. Lucy couldn't put her finger on it, but there was something about the grass that was just wrong. Same with those creepy trees, Lucy thought as she followed Oliver around to the backyard— where, at the edge of the tree line, stood a dilapidated two-car garage.

"It's not a garage," Oliver explained. "It's an old carriage house. You know, from back in the day when people rode horses."

The arched double doorways of the carriage house stood open, and half of the structure was covered entirely in branches—*Like giant hands*, Lucy thought, *trying to drag it into the woods.*

"*Def*-initely a hundred years old," Oliver said, his voice cracking. "And I'll bet you the property was bigger once, too."

"Why do you say that?"

"Look how those trees are growing. They weren't like that originally, I'm sure. If you were an arborist, you could go into the woods and figure out which trees were here when the land was cleared and which were not. Then you'd cut down one of the newer ones and count the *rings*." Oliver cleared his throat. "Anyway, that would give you a rough idea of how old the place is."

Lucy shrugged—she was only half listening now—and just stood there looking around anxiously as Oliver sauntered over to the carriage house and peered inside. Lucy didn't like the carriage house. Its darkened doorways reminded her of the hollow eyes of some monster peering up over the grass, and the branches were its hair. Oliver, on the other hand, didn't look frightened at all anymore. But that's how Oliver was. When he got into something—like comics and clocks and carriage houses—he forgot about the things that were bothering him.

But Lucy hadn't forgotten about what was bothering her. The place was too quiet. Yes, that was it, she realized. It was summer, which meant there should be loads of bugs buzzing and birds singing. But Lucy hadn't heard even a mosquito since they arrived. There was only the silence, broken now and then by the rustle of the wind in the trees.

As Oliver began poking around the carriage house, out of the corner of her eye, Lucy spied a large crow fluttering high among the branches to her right. She walked along the path to get a better look at it, and came to an area where the path forked off through the grass.

Lucy followed this second path a short distance and then stopped at the edge of the woods. If the crow was still around, she could no longer see it among the dark tangle of shadows overhead—but the path, she realized, kept going into the woods. It was littered with twigs and leaves, and at about twenty yards or so seemed to vanish altogether in the gloom. The branches bent over the top to form a tunnel, and Lucy began to wonder where such a path could possibly lead.

"What do you seek?" someone whispered.

Startled, Lucy whirled around expecting to find Oliver had sneaked up behind her. But her brother was still investigating the carriage house. Lucy could just make out his dim shape inside one of the doorways.

Her heart hammering, Lucy turned back toward the tunnel. A soft breeze moaned through the branches, swirling leaves toward her along the path and blowing back her bangs. Lucy caught the faintest whiff of what smelled like garbage, and then something cold and damp slithered over her foot.

Lucy shrieked and, scrambling backward, tripped and fell on her bottom. At the same time, a thick, knotted tree root bulged up alongside the path near the woods.

"What's the *matt*-er?" Oliver asked, rushing over. He helped Lucy to her feet. She was shivering, and the blood was pounding in her ears.

"That root there," Lucy said, pointing. "It—it touched my foot."

Oliver approached the root and kicked it. *Thump*. The root was solid, immovable. Oliver got down on his hands and knees and examined it more closely.

"You probably just got your foot caught," he said, stuffing his hand underneath, and Lucy saw that the root was raised an inch or two off the ground. But Lucy had been standing still when the root touched her, hadn't she?

"I swear I saw it move," Lucy muttered. "After I fell, I mean. And I know it wasn't there before."

"It probably just looked like it was moving. A trick of the light." Oliver stood up and clapped the dirt off his hands. "Still, we shouldn't go in there," he added, gazing down the path. "Not alone anyway. And not without a flashlight."

Oliver clicked his watch-flashlight on and off as Lucy blinked at the root in disbelief. Had it really bulged up from the ground? Or were the shadows playing tricks on her, as Oliver said, and the root had been there all along?

"But there was something else, too," Lucy said after a moment.

Oliver turned around with his eyebrows raised expectantly over his glasses, and suddenly Lucy felt stupid. Had she really heard a voice, or had she just imagined it? Maybe it was only the wind, whispering in the tunnel instead of moaning like it did before she got her foot caught under the root. Or had the root come first? Lucy wasn't so sure anymore. Everything now seemed fuzzy in her head.

"Never mind," she said, brushing the dirt off her buttocks. "But I'm telling you, that root moved."

"It could've been a snake coming out from *under* the root," Oliver said. "I don't think there are any poisonous ones around here, but still, we should be care—"

Oliver stopped and cocked his ear. Lucy heard it, too. A car pulling up out front.

"That must be Mr. Quigley," Oliver said. "Come on!"

This time, Oliver grabbed Lucy's wrist and led her around the house, where they found Mr. Quigley getting out of his car. Gone was the snazzy black suit he'd worn in the clock shop. The old man was dressed in plaid shorts, a yellow cardigan, and a tweed cap on his bandaged head. He looked as if he'd just stepped off the golf course, Lucy thought—but instead of clubs he carried a large, black ring of skeleton keys.

"Welcome, welcome," he said, beaming, and he shook hands with Mr. Tinker. "So wonderful to see you all again. I trust your journey was a pleasant one?"

As the adults made small talk about the trip, Lucy noticed that Mr. Quigley seemed nervous, his eyes darting back and forth between the house and her father.

"Anyhow, here are the keys to your summer abode," the old man said, moving toward the front steps. "I'm afraid I don't know which goes where. I've only owned the house for three months and—"

At that moment, a brick tumbled off the roof and landed on Mr. Quigley's car, shattering one of the headlights and bouncing off into the dirt. Everyone jumped, but Mr. Quigley was so startled, he broke out into a fit of coughing.

"Oh my goodness! Are you all right, Mr. Quigley?" asked Mr. Tinker, and the old man waved him away with his handkerchief.

"Perfectly fine," he said, pawing absently at the bandage beneath his cap. "I assure you, the house is in much better shape on the inside, but I do beg you to be careful out here. Especially you children when you're playing."

Mr. Tinker raked his fingers through his hair, staring anxiously at Mr. Quigley's shattered headlight. The old man seemed unconcerned about it, however, and moved around to the driver's side of his car, eager to leave.

"Well, then, I suppose I should let you get settled. Kitchen is fully stocked, and your bed linens are in the closet outside your quarters. Once you get your generator hooked up, I should think you'll find the place quite to your liking."

"Er—well—all right," stammered Mr. Tinker.

"Wish I could stay longer to show you around," said Mr. Quigley, looking at his watch. "But I have some pressing business that I must attend to before my trip—which now includes fixing a broken headlight."

Mr. Quigley chuckled and coughed into his handkerchief, then slipped back into his car, which Lucy realized had been running the entire time.

"I will check in on you in the morning," he called out the window, "but please feel free to call me should you need anything."

Mr. Quigley threw the car into reverse, turned, and,

kicking up a spray of dirt, disappeared into the woods at the end of the driveway.

"Er—right, then, let's get moving," said Mr. Tinker.

As her brother and father unloaded the truck, Lucy just stood there with her arms folded, watching the dust from Mr. Quigley's car settle as the sound of the engine faded into the silence—that horrible, heavy silence that Lucy already hated with all her heart.

FOUR

BLACKFORD HOUSE

"Well it *has* to be one of them," muttered Mr. Tinker, and he slipped another of the skeleton keys into the lock. He'd already tried nearly every one on the large iron ring, but still the front door wouldn't yield.

"Maybe the house doesn't want us here," Lucy said, shifting uncomfortably on her feet. "I bet you that's how Quigley hurt his head. The house threw a brick at him like it did at his car."

Oliver swallowed hard and changed his suitcase from one hand to the other. He really wished Lucy would stop saying things like that. The place was creepy enough without her making it worse.

Mr. Tinker rattled the key in the lock, jiggled the doorknob, and then—*click*—the key turned. "Victory," he said, sighing with relief. "Remind me to mark this one with some electrical tape, Ollie."

Oliver nodded, and Mr. Tinker opened the door.

Creeeeeak!

Oliver hung back in the doorway as Lucy and their father stepped into a cavernous, darkened foyer. Rectangles of dim, dusty light filtered in from the rooms on the other side, and Oliver could just make out a wide staircase dissolving up into the gloom at the far end of the foyer.

Mr. Tinker ran his hand along the wall and flipped a

switch. Nothing happened.

"You see?" he said, pointing up at the foyer's large chandelier. Its crystals glinted faintly in the shadows. "That's why Mr. Quigley needs the clock fixed before he moves in. It generates electricity for the entire house. How ingenious is that?"

Oliver pushed up his glasses, stepped inside, and set down his suitcase. His eyes had adjusted a bit, but with only the daylight streaming in, the foyer was still dim—in part because the walls were paneled three-quarters high in dark wood. To his left, he spied a shadowy parlor filled with antique furniture; to his right, a dining room with a long table. There were a handful of paintings on the walls, and where there was no paneling, the paper was peeled and gray.

"Well, will you look at that," said Mr. Tinker, gazing up the stairs. Built into the wall on the first landing was an enormous clock face that had to be at least ten feet in diameter. The hands, which were nearly as tall as the children themselves, had stopped at midnight (or noon, depending on your perspective, Oliver thought); and where the numbers should have been were twelve shallow, black holes.

"Let's have a look at our bread and butter," said Mr. Tinker, and the children followed him up the stairs to the clock—which was a *cuckoo clock*, Oliver discovered on closer inspection. There was a two-foot-high door for the cuckoo at the top, and the holes, which were about six inches deep, had been carved to look like animals.

"How cool!" Lucy said, reaching up to touch the hole where the *eight* should have been. It was shaped like a pig.

"Guess that gives new meaning to the phrase 'Ate like a pig,'" said Mr. Tinker, chuckling. "Get it? The number eight instead of *ate*?"

Lucy rolled her eyes, and Oliver stuck his hand into the hole for the *five*, which was shaped like a turtle. He could feel the curve of the animal's shell carved in hollow relief along the back of it.

"Anyhow, the detail is extraordinary," said Mr. Tinker, touching the *three* hole. It was shaped like a rabbit. The clock face itself was made up of dozens of white-painted bricks that were peeling in places; and Oliver could clearly make out below the cuckoo door, where the *twelve* should have been, a hole shaped like a cat. There was also a duck for the *two* and what looked like a rat or a mouse for the *seven*.

"But why would someone build a clock with holes in it shaped like animals?" Lucy asked.

"Maybe the animals are *miss*-ing," Oliver said, and he stood on his tippy-toes to touch the rabbit hole. "These holes remind me of statue niches—you know, like in a church or something. Besides, we've seen clocks like this before in the shop, right, Pop? Not this big, I mean, but with animals and stuff instead of numbers?"

Mr. Tinker nodded vaguely and opened a door that led to the clock's mechanical room. The only source of light inside was a round window in the back wall, but Oliver could see enough of the complex machinery to know this clock was unlike any they had ever come across in the shop. Oliver's mouth hung open in amazement.

"We'll need to take a closer look at this after we get the generator going," said his father. "What do you say we check out the rest of the house?"

The Tinkers climbed up the remainder of the stairs to the second floor, where they found four bedrooms off a dingy, dark-paneled hallway. Most of the furniture was covered in sheets, and the air smelled musty and stale. On the third floor, they found a cluttered attic that was much too dark to investigate, so they climbed back down to the first floor via a narrow servants' staircase that led to the kitchen.

On one side off the kitchen was the hallway that led to the servants' wing, and on the other, the door to the dining room. Inside, in addition to the long table he had seen earlier from the foyer, Oliver found a china-filled breakfront and a large buffet with a painting of Blackford House hung on the wall above it.

"Look how beautiful the house used to be," Lucy said.

Oliver thought the painting had to have been made

not long after the house was built. All the shutters were attached, the shingles and the chimneys were in perfect condition, and there were flowering gardens everywhere. There was also a horse-drawn carriage parked out front, and a white horse trotting around a field in the distance.

However, the biggest difference, Oliver thought, was the *color*. In the painting, everything looked bright and sunny. But in real life, even on a lovely summer day like today, Blackford House seemed to exist only in shades of gray.

"You were right, Oliver," Lucy said. "The property *was* a lot bigger. I don't see those creepy woods anywhere."

From the dining room, Mr. Tinker led the children back across the foyer and into the richly furnished parlor. There were more antiques than Oliver could count, as well as a massive stone fireplace, above which hung another painting—a large, dark portrait of a man and woman that likely had been damaged in a fire.

Oliver figured the painting was from the late 1800s— judging by the people's clothes. The woman was seated with the man standing behind her. Their skin was gray and their eyes sunken and dark—probably because of the smoke, Oliver concluded. The woman appeared to be hold- ing something—a child, perhaps—but Oliver could not be sure because there was only a large, black smudge in the woman's arms.

"What a creepy painting," Lucy muttered, staring up at it. "But it's kind of sad, too. The whole house, I mean. Don't you think, Pop?"

Mr. Tinker nodded absently and ran his fingers over an antique lamp that had grabbed his attention. Lucy frowned. *Poor kid*, Oliver thought. Pop never listened to her.

"I know what you mean, Lucy," Oliver said, looking around. "It's like, now that you've seen that painting, you can't help thinking about how the house used to be at the same time you're looking at it now."

"Yeah, I guess that's it," Lucy said glumly, and she slid open the doors to an adjoining room. "My solar panels!" she cried, her mood turning on a dime, and Oliver followed her into an enormous library with tall windows—the same tall windows they had seen before from outside. Below them was a faded, velvet-cushioned window seat, and built into the walls were dark wooden bookshelves crammed so high with books that rolling ladders had to be used to reach the ones at the top.

And it wasn't just a library, Oliver realized, but a *laboratory*, too. Off to one side, there was a long table cluttered with chemistry equipment; and directly behind it, the bookshelves were filled with all sorts of bottles and jars labeled with chemical symbols.

"How cute!" Lucy said, and she squatted down beside

two wooden statues near the fireplace. One was a lovable-looking dog, the other a snarling cat. Each was carved to look as if it were running—only the little dog was looking back over its shoulder as if the cat were chasing it.

"Did this mean cat hurt you?" Lucy asked, and she pulled out a small triangle of wood from between its teeth. "Look, it's his ear, Pop! The cat bit off this poor dog's ear!"

Lucy laid the ear against the dog's head. It was a perfect fit.

"Someone must've put it in the cat's mouth as a joke," said Mr. Tinker. "Maybe the other clocksmith Mr. Quigley tried."

"You think these could be some of the missing animals, Pop?" Lucy asked. "You know, the ones that go in the clock?"

Mr. Tinker shrugged and shook his head. "I doubt it, Lucy. They're the wrong shape for those niches and look to me like a set. Still, that's pretty funny, don't you think? Someone putting the dog's ear in the cat's mouth like that?"

Oliver pushed up his glasses and looked around.

There's nothing *funny about this place*, he thought.

No, nothing at all.

FIVE

TORSTEN

After a quick lunch of bologna sandwiches that Oliver had packed for them back home, the Tinkers spent the remainder of the afternoon settling in and readying their rooms in the servants' wing. They had very little to unpack, but lots to do.

Mr. Tinker took the first room off the kitchen, which had a single, unmade bed in which the previous clock-smith had slept—or at least that's what Mr. Tinker thought because the linens were stained and smelled of oil. He exchanged them for some fresh ones he found in the closet across the hall.

Lucy and Oliver took the room next door. It had two beds, but before making them, Lucy swept the floor and dusted the furniture while Oliver helped their father set up the generator outside. They were still busy with it when she was finished, so Lucy wandered first into the dining room to look at the painting of the house again and then into the library to look out her windows.

Yes, they were *her* windows, Lucy decided. At least for the summer. But maybe when the job was over, her father would have enough money to buy a house with windows just like these *for real*. The way the afternoon sunlight filtered in through them made Lucy feel warm and safe. And when she looked out at the woods, they didn't look nearly as creepy as before.

Maybe the windows were magical, Lucy thought. Or maybe she was just happy. Lucy knew from experience that, depending on whether you were happy or sad, the world could look different even when you weren't looking at it through ten-foot-tall windows.

Eventually, Lucy's eyes drifted to the wooden statue of the dog, which she'd set amid the chemistry equipment on the table before lunch. She'd set the ear there, too—no way she was going to give it back to the cat. Lucy did not like the cat. It was mean and ugly; and its eyes, which were made of black stones, seemed to follow her wherever she went. The dog's eyes were made of black stones, too, but unlike the cat, they looked lonely and sad.

"I'd be sad, too, if someone broke off my ear," Lucy said, and then she spotted a jar labeled Wood Glue on the table.

Impulsively, Lucy unscrewed the top and stuck her nose inside.

"Blech," she said, making a face. The glue looked like peanut butter and smelled like sour milk. But there was plenty left to repair the dog's ear.

Holding her breath and using a small glass stirrer that she found in a beaker nearby, Lucy carefully smeared the glue onto the dog's ear and stuck it back onto its head.

Then she set the dog on the window seat beneath the tall windows to dry.

"You rest there while your ear heals. Doctor's orders."

Lucy barked a reply for the dog and then frowned. She was too old to be playing make-believe with wooden animals—not to mention, if word ever got back to Betty Bigsby, the whole school would know about it. Betty was the meanest girl on the planet. Word on the street was that she and her fat brother, Theo, had been at the park looking for her yesterday. Too bad they didn't find her—Lucy would've been happy to give Betty another beating—but when she mentioned this to Oliver, he looked her square in the eyes and said, "You just stay away from the Bigsbys, you hear? Last thing you need is to be grounded all summer."

Lucy's eyes swiveled over to the mean-looking cat near the fireplace. "Yeah, you remind me of someone I know," she muttered, and impulsively carried the wooden statue upstairs to the clock. Her father was right. The hole where the *twelve* should have been was shaped for a cat sitting in profile, but the statue she was holding had been carved to look as if it were running, almost *leaping* for the dog. Maybe they were a set after all.

"Weird, though," Lucy muttered, bending over to look more closely at the hole for the dog, the *six*. It was the perfect size, shape, and depth for the wooden dog she'd found;

but it, too, was cut for an animal sitting in profile—totally different from the statue of the dog looking over its shoulder in the library.

Lucy sighed. Probably for the best—who wanted to see this cat's ugly mug every time they walked up the stairs? So Lucy began roaming about the house, looking for a place to hide it. She settled for a shelf in the broom closet, where she also returned the stuff she'd used to clean her bedroom. A moment later, the generator started up out back loudly enough to make the glassware in the kitchen cabinets rattle.

Lucy spent the remainder of the afternoon cleaning and helping run power cords from the generator to the appliances in the kitchen, as well as up into the clock's mechanical room—where, much to her father's surprise, he found a work light and a set of tools left by the previous clocksmith. Lucy thought he looked worried, but when she asked Oliver about it later, he explained that their father just needed time to figure out how the clock worked. It was unlike any clock they had ever seen. Lucy didn't bother asking him why. Even if Oliver told her, she wouldn't know the difference.

After that, Lucy helped her brother fix a supper of clam chowder and corn bread with the food Mr. Quigley had stocked for them. Most of the food was canned, and the rest was the dried, just-add-water kind people used when they went camping. There was even powdered milk, which Lucy hadn't known existed but which she thought tasted wonderful.

In fact, Lucy couldn't remember having eaten so well, nor could she remember a time when it felt so good to be together as a family. True, the house was spooky when it got dark, even after Lucy's father turned on a bunch of battery-powered lanterns Mr. Quigley had given them. They cast strange, shifting shadows on the walls that reminded Lucy of ghosts. And when she thought about spending a whole summer without the internet and TV, Lucy got a tense, panicky feeling in her stomach.

"Think of it as an adventure," her father said. After all, it was a new beginning for them. And what was a new beginning if not an adventure?

Lucy thought she understood what her father meant, especially after supper when they all played an epic game of Monopoly at the kitchen table. Her father had packed it along with some other games that Lucy hadn't known how to play. She lost, but still it was fun; and her father promised that they would do things like this more often when they got home. This gave Lucy a tingly feeling of excitement and hope; and if that was what being on an adventure felt like, then it wasn't so bad.

Later that night, however, when she crawled into bed

and Oliver turned off the lantern on the nightstand, Lucy did not like being on an adventure at all. She was scared, of course, being in this big strange house with the wind whistling all around—not to mention she could still see that scary tunnel in the woods outside her window. But even worse, Lucy felt all sorts of sad and lonely.

Lucy closed her eyes and imagined her windows in the library, hoping that they would make her feel safe and warm like they did when she was looking at them for real. But soon her thoughts drifted to the statue of the little dog. The poor thing had looked scared and sad and lonely, too.

Suddenly, more than anything, Lucy wanted the little dog by her side—but there was no way she was going through this big dark house all alone to get it. Lucy flicked on the lantern and asked Oliver if he would come with her to the library. She wanted to see if the little dog's ear was dry, she told him.

"Why the heck do you need to do that *now*?" he asked, sitting up and squinting. Lucy shrugged—she didn't have an answer—but Oliver sighed and put on his glasses as if she'd answered him anyway.

Using the flashlight in his watch, Oliver led Lucy through the darkened house and into the library, where she picked up the little dog from the window seat and brought it back to their bedroom. Oliver didn't give her a hard time when she laid down with the statue in her bed. He always seemed to understand when Lucy needed him to let her be.

"Just be careful you don't roll over and hurt yourself," he said, crawling back into bed. "It's not a stuffed animal, you know."

Oliver switched off the lantern, and the children exchanged their good nights. Lucy tucked the little dog under her arm and closed her eyes. The window was open, and she could hear the wind rattling the branches outside. With the little dog by her side, Lucy wasn't scared of the tunnel in the woods anymore. Well, maybe just a little.

Lucy pulled the dog closer. Someday, she thought, when they moved into their new house with the big windows, her father would get her a real dog. Until then, a wooden dog would have to do. And it would need a name, of course. However, before she could think of one, Lucy fell asleep and began to dream. Or at least she *thought* she did; for what happened next *had* to have been a dream.

"Wake up, miss!" someone whispered in her ear, and Lucy felt a tickling sensation, like wet sandpaper, against her cheek. Her eyes fluttered open, and for a moment she had no idea where she was. The room was silver with moonlight and filled with unfamiliar shapes and shadows.

"Please, Miss Lucy, I need to get back!"

Lucy turned her head on her pillow and found the little

dog, eyes wide and tongue lolling, hovering over her. It licked her cheek, and Lucy bolted upright.

The little dog was alive!

"Don't be afraid, miss," it said, backing away on the bed. "I just need you to open the door for me so I can get back to our hiding spot!"

Lucy just sat there, eyes blinking and mouth hanging open.

"I must be dreaming," she muttered, and the little dog moved closer again.

"No, you're not, Miss Lucy," he whispered. "You're the new caretaker."

"Caretaker?"

"Well, you took care of me, didn't you?" the dog said, wiggling his repaired ear. "But if Meridian finds out you brought me near an open window, she'll never believe you're on our side. Open windows are against the rules!"

"What are you talking about? Who's Meridian? And who are *you*?"

"My name is Torsten Six," said the little dog, wagging his tail. "And Meridian is the cat who had my car in her mouth."

"But you're just . . . *statues*. And statues don't talk—or bite—or—"

"We can do all those things—but only after midnight.

61

Meridian thinks it's because that's when our magic is the most powerful. After midnight, we can go back and forth between being alive and wooden just by thinking about it. See?"

Torsten closed his eyes, and when he opened them again, his pupils were black stones and his body had hardened into wood. Lucy gasped, and then the statue's eyes blinked, and Torsten became real again.

"Neat, isn't it?" he said. "Except when the sun comes up, we can't do that. We have to remain statues until midnight whether we want to or not."

"But—I don't understand."

"Neither do we, really. This is all new to us—been going on ever since the clock stopped—which is why Meridian and I got caught in the library." Torsten's stomach growled. "It was all my fault. I was only trying to find us food. None of us has eaten in days, and I was *so* hungry. I thought I had more time before sunrise—and Meridian was only trying to pull me back again—and then, *rip*, off came my ear. That's something else that's new to us—*eating*. We never had to do that when we were in the clock."

"Wait—so you and Meridian *do* belong in the clock?"

Torsten nodded.

"But I tried putting you back in your holes and—"

"Again, that's my fault. We froze in different positions

at sunrise so we don't fit anymore. And since your father and brother saw us, we have to stay that way until—" Torsten turned his head to the door. "Oh, it's all my fault! I should've never left the hiding spot!"

"Hiding spot? What are you hiding from?"

As Torsten opened his mouth to speak, the wind moaned loudly through the trees outside. The little dog flinched and shivered.

"*Please*, Miss Lucy," he whined. "There's no time to explain! I need to get back. It's too dangerous for me to be roaming about. And if something happens—if Meridian finds out that the window was open and you got me snatched, she'll never believe you're the new caretaker—"

Just then, Oliver stirred in his bed. "Lucy, shut up," he mumbled groggily. He was facing the wall, just a big gray lump under his sheets. Lucy could see the rise and fall of his chest, and when his breathing became slow and steady, she turned back to Torsten.

But the little dog was wooden again, his body in the same position as when she'd first found him in the library. Lucy growled in frustration and shook him.

"Torsten, wake up!"

"Lucy!" Oliver groaned, rolling over to face her. His eyes were only smudges of shadow in the moonlight, but Lucy could tell they were open. "What are you doing?"

"Er—nothing," Lucy said, setting Torsten back down on the bed beside her. "I guess I was dreaming."

"Well, lie down and go to sleep." Oliver checked his watch on the nightstand. "It's after midnight."

The wind moaned again outside. Lucy shivered, and her heart began to beat very fast. She quickly slipped out of bed and closed the window.

"What did you do that for?" Oliver asked.

"I'm chilly," Lucy lied. Even though Oliver was the most understanding person on the planet, she didn't quite know how to explain to him what had just happened. If she had been dreaming, it was the most vivid, real dream she had ever had. If she *hadn't* been dreaming, then only one of two things was possible: either the wooden statues she had found in the library were magical, or she was going bonkers.

All this ran through Lucy's mind in a millisecond. And as Oliver rolled over to face the wall again, she got back into bed and lay there with the statue of Torsten on her chest, staring into his black stone eyes for what seemed like hours until, eventually, Oliver began to snore.

"The coast is clear now," Lucy whispered, so quietly that she could barely even hear herself. But the little dog's eyes showed no signs of life, and his position remained the same as before.

Well, not exactly, Lucy thought. It was hard to tell for

sure in the moonlight, but Torsten's shoulders seemed a bit lower now, and his head wasn't turned as far around as when he'd been looking at the cat. His ears looked more relaxed, too; and best of all, his eyes weren't nearly as scared and sad and lonely as before.

Lucy tucked the statue under her arm again. "I'll protect you," she whispered, closing her eyes. Lucy was certain Torsten could hear her. After all, he'd known her name and that she'd fixed his ear.

Unless, of course, the whole thing had been a dream.

Dream or no dream, Lucy felt strangely safe and warm with the dog there by her side—like she did when she stood in the light from her windows in the library. Maybe this place *was* magical after all. Lucy hoped so. But either way, she thought, there was nothing to be afraid of.

At least, not yet.

SIX

THE BOY IN THE WOODS

The next morning, Oliver awoke to find Lucy fast asleep with the little dog tucked under her arm. They were both too old to be sleeping with stuffed animals, never mind *wooden* ones, but Oliver could sympathize. It *was* a little scary sleeping alone in such a big house after sleeping for so long in the same bed back home.

Oliver quietly dressed and slipped across the hallway into the bathroom, where he found a new zit blazing back at him in the mirror. It was on his chin, making the grand total there six. Oliver's heart sank. He had secretly hoped that the fresh air in Rhode Island would work wonders for his complexion, but so far, no dice. The fact that there was only cold water in Blackford House wasn't going to help things either.

Oliver pressed his lips together tightly and washed his face—superheroes didn't feel sorry for themselves about zits and living with no hot water. Then he brushed his teeth and padded out into the kitchen, where he found his father eating a bowl of cereal over the sink. Oliver informed him that Lucy wasn't awake yet. "She had a bad *dream*," he said, voice cracking with his first words of the day. "Didn't sleep well, I think."

"Poor kid," said Mr. Tinker. "We'll wait to turn on the generator, then."

Oliver wolfed down his own bowl of cereal and then accompanied his father up into the clock. The morning sun hit the mechanical room's tiny, round window in such a way that there was no need for the work lights. But still, Oliver's father was as confused as ever by the clock's machinery. Oliver, too.

On the surface, it appeared to be just a giant version of the kind of cuckoo mechanism they had seen a hundred times in the shop, complete with a scissor armature and an extension arm that pushed the cuckoo bird through the door. But like the animals that fit into the holes around the clock face, the cuckoo bird was missing, too.

"And yet, there's no winding mechanism," Mr. Tinker muttered, scratching his head. Oliver understood. If there was no winding mechanism, no wheels and springs and gears to make the clock tick, then what did?

"It must have something to do with the pipes," said Mr. Tinker. That was the thing that had befuddled them from the start: pipes inside a clock—all of which zigzagged from one of the walls to a central iron sphere about the size of a basketball. The sphere itself appeared to be part of the pendulum mechanism.

Oliver ducked under and around the pipes to the place where they had been bolted to the wall. It was made entirely of dark wood. "Where do you think they go, Pop?"

Oliver asked—*knock, knock, knock.* The wall felt solid, like knocking on a tree.

Mr. Tinker shrugged, and as he began examining the pendulum, Oliver squeezed around the pipes to the rear of the clock face—the bricks for which, unlike the outside of the clock, had been left in their natural color. Black.

Oliver turned on his watch-flashlight and studied the rear of the clock face more closely. There were twelve pipe couplings around the perimeter, one on the back of each niche, and between them, the faint outline of where the pipes had once connected the animals in a circle. At the bottom of the circle, on the back of the *six* hole, there was a coupling with a third opening for a pipe extending out toward the machinery.

Oliver moved back to the iron sphere, and sure enough found another coupling that could have, at one time, received the pipe from the *six* hole. This coupling had been capped, however, and a new coupling had been welded to the opposite side of the sphere, out of which four zigzagging pipes had been haphazardly bolted to the wooden wall.

"Hey, Pop. I think the guy before us rerouted all these pipes into the wall here. Looks like they originally connected to the back of the clock face."

Oliver's father nodded absently and then leaned all his weight against the pendulum rod. It wouldn't budge. "Come help me with this, Ollie. I think this thing is jammed."

Oliver joined him, and they pushed with all their might. The space was cramped, with barely enough room for the two of them, but then Oliver felt the rod give slightly.

"Now pull!" said his father. They did, and the rod gave a little the other way. Gears squeaked, and then Oliver heard a low groan, like the sound of straining tree limbs, coming from deep within the walls.

Oliver and his father let go of the rod and listened. Had the groan come from inside the walls or outside? Oliver couldn't tell now. The window was open, but the groaning had stopped.

Red-faced and dizzy, Mr. Tinker leaned against the pendulum rod for support. Oliver hitched in his breath, and his heart began to hammer.

"You o-*kay*, Pop?" he said, voice cracking, and his father waved him away.

"Ollie, I'm fine. Just a little light-headed—"

"Did you bring your high blood pressure medicine? You need to sit down?"

Oliver's father smiled. "I'm *fine*. Like anyone else, I just need to remember to breathe when I exert myself. That's why I got light-headed."

"Yeah, but you *did* take your medicine, right?"

"Ollie, listen," said his father, holding him by the

shoulders. "Nothing is going to happen to me, you understand? I'm not going anywhere."

Embarrassed, Oliver dropped his eyes to the floor. In the first few months after he'd lost his mother, Oliver worried *a lot* about losing his father, too—so much so that he had to start seeing a counselor because he didn't want to be away from him at school. The counselor didn't help, but working with his father in the clock shop did. Oliver didn't worry now nearly as much as he used to. But still, at times like these, what with his father's high blood pressure and all . . .

"Your mother would be proud of you," he said, gazing down at Oliver fondly. "The man you're becoming, the way you've taken on so much responsibility for the family—" Mr. Tinker's voice was tight with emotion. He cleared his throat and smiled. "Anyhow, I'm one thing you *don't* need to worry about, okay? Remember what I told you." He mussed Oliver's hair. "All that worrying is a vicious cycle."

Oliver smiled and nodded.

"All right, let's get that generator going," said Mr. Tinker. "I need more light to see how the timing module connects to the pendulum."

Oliver bounded down the stairs, through the kitchen, and out the back door to the generator—which, for safety's sake, his father had set a few yards away from the house on the path leading to the woods.

Oliver disconnected the power cords they had been using the day before (his father always did this first so nothing would blow up) and then checked the generator's tank. It was almost dry, so he tromped through the grass toward the carriage house, where the gas cans were stored. He was about halfway there when he noticed that something about the carriage house looked different. Oliver stopped.

The branches. There were more of them now.

Yesterday, on the right side of the carriage house, he could see about a third of the wall. But now it was almost entirely covered, and a few of the branches had even curled around into the doorway as if they meant to pull the carriage house apart.

Trees don't grow that fast, Oliver told himself, so he decided that the branches had probably just shifted during the night. After all, it *had* been a bit windy—a spooky, moaning kind of windy that had made the back of his neck prickle.

Oliver swallowed hard and hurried into the carriage house. In addition to the gas cans, there was some scrap wood and black stones, a couple of wooden ladders, and some rusty old gardening tools. Oliver grabbed the nearest gas can and ran back to the generator. He filled the tank, closed the generator's choke, and was about to grab the pull chain when someone whispered:

"What do you seek?"

Oliver whirled to find a boy standing at the mouth of the tunnel in the woods. He was pale, with black hair and eyes, and was dressed in dark clothes that reminded Oliver of the old-fashioned hunting outfits people wore in the movies. The boy wore boots, too, and a tweed cap like the one Mr. Quigley had on the day before. He appeared to be the same age as Oliver, but it was hard to tell. Even in the early-morning sun, the edge of the woods was all shadow.

Oliver pushed up his glasses and blinked at the boy blankly.

"I *said*, good morning," the boy said, smiling. Oliver was certain that the boy had said something else, but now he couldn't remember.

"Good morning," Oliver said warily.

"My name is Teddy. What's yours?"

"Oliver."

"Well, that's a *twist*, isn't it?" Teddy said, chuckling, but again, Oliver only blinked. "You've never heard of Oliver Twist? As in the story by Charles Dickens?" Oliver nodded vaguely, and Teddy frowned. "Let me guess, you're the son of the new clocksmith Mr. Quigley hired, aren't you?"

"Oh, you know Mr. *Quig*-ley?" Oliver cleared his throat, embarrassed. Stupid voice cracking.

"I should say so," Teddy said. "Mr. Quigley fired my

father. He used to be the caretaker here before that old devil bought the place. Even tried to fix that clock for him."

"Oh, so your father was the previous clocksmith?"

Teddy nodded and smiled bitterly. "And *your* father is the current one."

Oliver thrust his hands into the pockets of his jeans. He couldn't put his finger on it, but there was something about this Teddy kid that was *off*. He sounded British, like Mr. Quigley. But even stranger, he seemed both hostile and friendly at the same time.

"Anyhow, we live in the old caretaker's cottage," Teddy said, jerking his thumb behind him. "Only a couple hundred yards into the woods and not too far from Hollow Pond. Good fishing there, if you're into that sort of thing."

Oliver wasn't sure if he was into fishing or not. He'd never been.

"I didn't know there was a pond around here," he said, moving closer, but he couldn't see much past Teddy in the gloom.

"There are a couple of creeks, too," Teddy said, looking left and right. "They branch off on either side of the pond and then link up on the western side of the property. Not too far from the bridge you crossed to get here. The Shadow Woods sit in the middle of it all, surrounded by water on all sides, like a big wedge of pie—although the

Shadow Woods aren't that big. Only a hundred acres or so."

"Shadow Woods?" Oliver said, and Teddy looked up at the branches.

"Self-explanatory, I should think. Legend has it these woods are magical." Teddy narrowed his eyes and smiled mischievously. "Matter of fact, Blackford House is *built* from shadow wood. So, I suppose that makes it magical, too."

"Yeah, right," Oliver said, chuckling. Teddy's smile dropped, and his eyes grew sad. A soft, moaning breeze rustled the leaves on the path behind him, and Oliver caught a whiff of something rotten and garbagy.

"We mock what we don't understand, Oliver Tinker," Teddy said quietly.

"How did you know my last name?" Oliver asked, his heart suddenly beating very fast, and then his father called, *"Hey, forest ranger!"*

Startled, Oliver spun around and spied his father's head poking out of the mechanical room window about halfway up the side of house. A long power cord extended down from the window to the generator. Oliver's father jiggled it.

"What's taking you so long? he asked.

"Sorry, I'm *com*-ing!" Oliver called, and his father ducked his head inside again. Oliver turned back to Teddy to say goodbye, but the boy had vanished.

Oliver stepped to the edge of the woods, where the

flagstones ended and the leaf-strewn, tunnel-like path began. The garbagy smell was gone, and as Oliver's eyes probed the darkness, he could see no sign of Teddy anywhere.

But there was something on the ground where the boy had been standing.

Oliver bent down and picked it up.

It was a large black acorn.

SEVEN

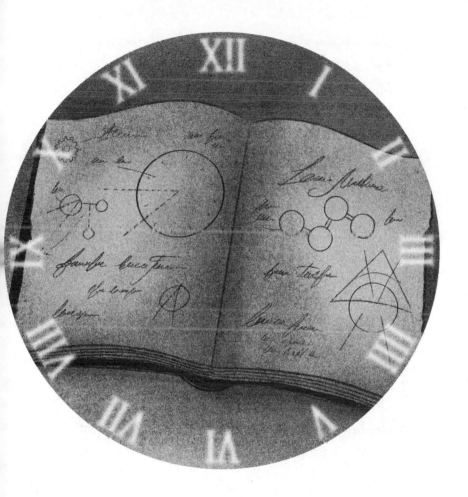

THE CROW TAKES NOTICE

Bar-rumpa—bar-rumpa—bar-rumpa-num—rumpa-num-rumpa-num!

The longest day of Lucy Tinker's life began with the sound of the generator startling her awake.

She immediately felt for Torsten, who was still lying wooden beside her. The little dog could only come alive after midnight, he'd told her, and then turned back into a statue at sunrise. So why hadn't he come alive again after Oliver went back to sleep? Or, for that matter, after she did?

Maybe Oliver had scared Torsten so much that he didn't want to risk waking him up again. Torsten had been scared enough already, especially of the open window. And then there was all that other stuff he'd been going on about: Meridian and the hiding spot and getting snatched? It didn't make sense.

Then again, that's the way dreams usually were. They didn't make sense.

"But it wasn't a dream," Lucy muttered, gazing into Torsten's shiny black eyes. Dreams were fuzzy and far away the next morning, and by the time you brushed your teeth you'd practically forgotten all about them. Unless they were superweird or scary. True, the encounter with Torsten *was* superweird—and maybe *a little* scary—but still . . .

Lucy swung her feet onto the floor, rubbed the sand

from her eyes, then checked Oliver's compass-watch on the nightstand. *9:47*—which meant she had just over *fourteen hours* before Torsten would come alive again. Lucy groaned impatiently. She had so much to ask the little dog, but also so much to tell him.

And then an idea occurred to her.

"If you can hear me, maybe Meridian can, too," Lucy said—that is, if the cat hadn't gone back to the hiding spot. Either way, there would be no talking to them here in the bedroom with the generator going. Lucy could hardly hear herself think.

Lucy snatched a T-shirt and shorts from the dresser, changed and washed in the bathroom, and then brought Torsten out with her into the kitchen, where she unlatched the broom closet and peeked inside. Meridian's eyes twinkled back at her in the dim shaft of light from the door, and Lucy exhaled with relief. The cat was still on the shelf where she'd left her, but Lucy noticed some sawdust and what looked like claw marks on the inside bottom of the door. Could it be that the cat had tried to get out during the night and return to the hiding spot?

Lucy carefully took down Meridian from the shelf and, tucking her under one arm and Torsten under the other, grabbed an open box of Froot Loops from the counter with her teeth and hurried into the library. She set the animals down on the window seat, turned a big leather armchair to face them, and then closed the library's sliding pocket doors. The generator now was only a low drone in the distance.

Lucy sat down across from the animals with her box of Froot Loops and popped a couple into her mouth. *I'm the only Froot Loop here,* she thought, *talking like a crazy person to wooden animals.* But that's exactly what Lucy did. She started talking.

"Hello, Meridian," Lucy said. "My name is Lucy Tinker. Er—nice to meet you."

The cat stared back at her hatefully with its shiny black eyes and its snarling fanged mouth. Lucy gulped. Her heart was suddenly beating very fast; and when she popped some more Froot Loops into her mouth, they tasted so dry and cardboardy that she could barely swallow them.

"Er—anyway," Lucy began again, "my father, Charles Tinker, was hired by Mr. Quigley to fix the clock here. Torsten thinks I'm the new caretaker, but I don't know what that means. Don't get me wrong, I'm happy to take care of both of you while we're here this summer. My brother's name is Oliver, by the way. He's a good kid. All of us are. Good, I mean."

Lucy wasn't sure if her mind was playing tricks on her, but Meridian's eyes seemed narrower—more suspicious now than hateful—and one corner of her mouth was higher than the other, so that her snarl looked more like a sneer.

"I'm telling you the truth," Lucy said. "We mean you no harm. I didn't know about the open-window rule, but I do now. Torsten told me. It was my fault that he didn't return to the hiding spot, so don't be angry with him. And don't be angry with me for putting you in that broom closet. I didn't know that you came alive and that you belonged in the clock and—"

Lucy stopped. There was still so much that she didn't know. Torsten had been afraid of something, but what?

As if in answer to her question, a large crow suddenly swooped down in front of the library windows. Startled, Lucy sent the box of Froot Loops flying. The big black bird hovered there for a moment, studying the wooden animals closely, and then without warning seemed to try to snatch them through the glass.

Lucy shrieked and scooped up the animals, shielding them with her body in the chair as the crow's talons went *thump-scratch-thump* against the windowpanes.

"Get away from them!" Lucy cried, and the crow backed away, beating its wings and training its black eyes on Lucy for a moment. And then with a loud *"Caw!"* the big black bird flew off—its cries quickly fading beneath the distant drone of the generator.

Lucy sat there frozen with her heart hammering and the wooden animals clutched to her chest. They were shivering. Or was Lucy just imagining it because *she* was shivering?

"It's all right, he's gone." Lucy gently set the animals on the chair and, moving to the window seat, gazed out at the woods. There was no sign of the crow anywhere—only the trees, black and twisted, looming beyond the overgrown grass.

"He's the one you're afraid of, isn't he?" Lucy asked, turning back to the animals. "That's why open windows are against the rules. That's why you were worried about getting snatched, Torsten. The crow. How many of you has he taken? And how many of you are left?"

The animals stared back at Lucy silently—Meridian's stone eyes hateful and glaring; Torsten's eyes sad and afraid. And now there was a crow, a *real* crow thrown into the mix. But why was it taking the animals?

Lucy slipped off the window seat and—*crunch!*—stepped barefooted on some Froot Loops she'd dropped on the floor. "Blech!" she said, brushing the crumbs off the bottoms of her feet; but Lucy didn't have much of an appetite left anyway. The animals, on the other hand, hadn't eaten in days. That's how they got caught in the library in the first place, Torsten had said. He'd been looking for something to eat when Meridian tried to drag him back into their hiding spot.

"Their hiding spot," Lucy muttered, looking around. It had to be in here somewhere—or at least close by.

Lucy brushed off the rest of the crumbs from her feet, scooped what she could back into the box, and then tossed the whole thing into a nearby wastebasket. She would need to sweep the rest, but what was she going to do with Meridian and Torsten all day? She must hide them somewhere safe until midnight, Lucy thought, at which time she would give them some food from the pantry and ask them questions.

Lucy carried the animals back to the broom closet, where she hid them on a shelf behind some old boxes of lightbulbs. "Don't worry," she whispered, "I'll come back for you at midnight with some food." Then Lucy grabbed a dustpan and brush and headed back to the library.

She had just finished sweeping up the rest of the cereal crumbs when she noticed a leather book on the floor near the chemistry table. *Must have fallen off during the chaos,* Lucy thought, although she didn't remember seeing it before.

Lucy thumbed through the book and quickly discovered it was an old journal belonging to someone named Roger Blackford. It was filled mostly with boring notes about scientific experiments, complete with formulas and mathematical equations that Lucy couldn't begin to understand.

But there was one entry toward the end of the journal that did manage to grab her attention.

"*19 April, 1908,*" Lucy read. "*Although Abigail and I promised each other never to speak of our son again, in the interest of our alchemy, on this, the anniversary of his death, I am compelled to document what has happened. For the last year, the paintings of our son have been slowly turning black. Abigail, still grief stricken, refuses to take them down or even talk about it. However, I am certain that nothing in our collective knowledge could account for such a phenomenon. I intend to make some adjustments to the clock to determine if our son's demise has affected the balance, and yet I suspect the house itself is to blame—for some time now it has been becoming more sentient. Should I determine the cause, I shall document it here. If not, I shall honor my promise to Abigail and never speak of our son again. —RB.*"

"*RB* stands for Roger Blackford," Lucy muttered, thumbing through the rest of the journal. More formulas and notes on experiments—but nothing about the paintings or the Blackfords' son.

Just then, the sound of a car horn startled Lucy from her thoughts, and she tossed the journal on the chemistry table. Lucy ran into the parlor and gazed out the window. It was Mr. Quigley. The old man stood beside his car at the end of the driveway, peeking out from underneath an umbrella. Lucy frowned. She had only been kidding the day before when she said the house had thrown that brick at Mr. Quigley's car. But now, after reading that journal . . .

Lucy swiveled her eyes up to the painting above the hearth. The man and the woman were Roger and Abigail Blackford. And the black smudge in Abigail's arms was their son. Something bad must have happened to him. And not only that, Roger Blackford thought the house itself was to blame for damaging the paintings.

Honk, honk, honk!

Mr. Quigley was reaching through his car window, Lucy saw, so she dashed into the foyer and called for her father. He and Oliver emerged from the clock a second later, and then everyone hurried outside. The headlight on Mr. Quigley's car was still broken, Lucy noticed, but no one mentioned it.

Mr. Quigley smiled out from under his umbrella and, adjusting the bandage on his head, shot a nervous glance up at the house. "Forgive the umbrella," he said. "But my head felt a little too sore today for a hat. Doctor's orders. Don't want to get too much sun."

"How *did* you hurt your head, Mr. Quigley?" Lucy asked.

"Er—well—" he stammered. "I bumped it getting into my car. Always been a bit clumsy, I'm afraid." Mr. Quigley chuckled and coughed into his handkerchief. "Add a summer cold into the mix and— Well, anyhow, I trust your first evening here in Watch Hollow was a pleasant one?"

"Very pleasant, thank you, yes," said Mr. Tinker. "But you weren't kidding about that clock. I've never seen anything like it."

Mr. Quigley smiled. "The former clocksmith made great strides in directing the energy from the shadow wood, the magnetic current from which, when transferred through the pendulum, provides electricity for the house. I'm no engineer, of course, but if I recall correctly, it was the pendulum mechanism that was giving him the trouble."

"See, I told you that was the problem, Ollie," said Mr. Tinker, and Lucy noticed for the first time that her brother looked uneasy. "Seems to me the most sensible solution is to outfit the clock with a winding mechanism to get that pendulum moving. Then it will conduct the magnetic energy from the—er—what did you call it? Shadow wood?"

Mr. Quigley chuckled and waved his hand dismissively.

"The Shadow Woods are what the locals call the forest here—which, incidentally, came with the property when I bought it. The house and its clock were built over a hundred years ago from these trees. A family by the name of Blackford."

Lucy's heart skipped a beat. So Roger and Abigail Blackford were the original builders of the house.

"In any event," Mr. Quigley went on, "I acquired the house from a distant relative of the Blackfords in England. It had been abandoned for decades, ever since Abigail Blackford died in the early nineteen eighties. She was over a hundred years old, mind you. Since that time, the house had been looked after by a management company hired by the gentleman from whom I bought it. And yet no one can tell me exactly when the clock stopped and why."

"Well, Mr. Quigley, the clock certainly is a marvel of technical wizardry—"

"It looks like those pipes used to connect to the back of the clock face," Oliver said, interrupting his father. "Do you think maybe that's why it isn't working?"

Mr. Quigley smiled nervously. "Er—no—" he stammered, peeking up at the house again from under his umbrella. "I'm afraid that was something the previous clocksmith tried. He rerouted the pipes into the clock face and— Well, let's just say the effect was disastrous. He almost blew up the entire house. Which is why, once he reconnected the pipes to the shadow wood, I had to dismiss him."

"What about the animals?" Lucy asked, and every-one looked at her as if she had three heads. Lucy blushed. "Well—er—I mean, obviously there used to be animals in the clock instead of numbers. I was just wondering what happened to them."

"I honestly don't know," said Mr. Quigley. "However, you needn't worry about replacing them. Merely decorative elements, I assure you, and unimportant to the clock's power. Which reminds me"—Mr. Quigley reached through the car window and popped the trunk—"I brought you some more gas for that generator of yours."

"Perfect, we were running low. Ollie, bring those cans into the carriage house, will you? And you can shut the generator off, too. We'll be breaking for lunch soon."

Lucy thought her brother looked disappointed now. He pushed up his glasses and, with a nod, fetched the gas cans from Mr. Quigley's trunk and disappeared with them around the house.

"Well then, I'm happy to see things are going smoothly," said Mr. Quigley, and then he turned his eyes on Lucy. "And you, Miss Lucy, how have you been passing your time so far in your summer abode?"

There was something about the way Mr. Quigley was looking at her that made Lucy uneasy—almost as if the old man knew she had been spending her morning talking to wooden animals and reading Roger Blackford's journal. And yet, out here in the sunlight, the idea that a house could have magical animals that came alive at midnight seemed crazy. Maybe she was letting her imagination run away with her; maybe she had only dreamed about Torsten after all. Either way, she wasn't ready to talk about it.

Lucy stuffed her hands in her pockets and, with a shrug, looked away.

"Lucy here has always been able to keep herself occupied," said her father, and then the generator was heard sputtering to a stop out back. "That reminds me—er—why don't you run along now and see what Oliver is up to, Lucy. I need to speak to Mr. Quigley about some business. You guys can get some playtime in before lunch."

Lucy said goodbye to Mr. Quigley and ran around to the back of the house, her eyes darting up at the trees in search of the crow. She did not see the big black bird anywhere, but found Oliver standing at the edge of the woods where the tunnel was. He flicked her a halfhearted wave and Lucy joined him—the two of them just standing there in silence, gazing into the woods as a soft breeze whispered through the branches.

"I met the son of the former clocksmith this morning," Oliver said finally. "He was actually the caretaker of the place until Mr. Quigley fired him. The father, I mean."

"Caretaker?" Lucy said, her heart suddenly beating fast. That's what Torsten had called *her*. The new caretaker.

"*Yeah*," Oliver said, his voice cracking. "They live in a cottage a couple hundred yards into the woods, Teddy said. That's the kid's name. Being that Mr. Quigley owns these woods, I guess he's allowing them to stay on until Teddy's father finds another job or something."

Lucy didn't reply and began fiddling with her braid. Her mind was spinning now. *Caretaker?*

"That's nice of Mr. Quigley, don't you think? I mean, the guy almost blew up his house, he said."

Lucy shrugged. She didn't know where Oliver was going with this and began struggling with whether to tell him about Torsten and the crow. Oliver would want to see for himself, but the crow was nowhere to be found, and the wooden animals wouldn't come alive again until midnight. However, given the way Torsten reacted to Oliver the night before, they might not come alive at all when he was around—or at least, not until they knew they could trust him. And even though Torsten thought Lucy was the new caretaker, who knew what Meridian thought? Lucy hoped that she had won her over earlier in the library, but she wouldn't know for sure until midnight.

"You know what I mean?" Oliver asked.

"Huh—what?" Lucy said, blinking back at him. She'd been so wrapped up in her thoughts, she hadn't heard a word he'd said. Oliver sighed.

"It's not a normal clock is all I'm saying. Just like the Shadow Woods are not normal woods."

Lucy shivered and folded her arms. She did not like that

name. Shadow Woods.

"I was thinking about asking Teddy's father what went *wrong*," Oliver said, cracking, and he cleared his throat and thrust his hands into his pockets.

"The guy that almost blew up the house? He'd be the *last* person I'd ask."

"You don't understand, Lucy. From what I can tell, it makes sense that Teddy's father would've tried to reroute those pipes into the clock face."

"Well, I think it's a dumb idea." Lucy jerked her chin at the tunnel. "And I think it's even a dumber idea to go looking for this Teddy kid's father *in there*. Shadow Woods. Can you think of a creepier name? Maybe Death Woods, but still—promise me you won't ever go in there, okay? I don't like these woods at all."

Oliver smiled. "They can't be *that* bad if Teddy and his father live in them. Teddy even said there's a pond in there that has great fishing."

"We don't fish."

Oliver chuckled and rubbed his brow, thinking. "Okay, maybe it *is* a dumb idea," he said, and Lucy noticed that he'd smeared black stuff all over his forehead. Lucy pointed it out, and Oliver, confused, checked his hands and then his pockets. He scooped what looked like a clump of ash out of one of them.

"What the—?" he said, smelling his fingers. "I found an acorn earlier and put it in my pocket. I must have crushed it or something when I was working in the clock."

Oliver tried dusting his hands off together, but it only made matters worse, and soon both of his hands were completely black.

"Great, now it's starting to itch, too," he said, scratching at the pimples on his forehead, and Lucy giggled.

"You're such a spaz," she said. "Come on, let's get you cleaned up."

Lucy took her brother's wrist and was about to lead him back toward the house when the sight of the clock room window stopped her in her tracks. It was open.

"What's the matter?" Oliver asked, but Lucy didn't know how to tell him about the no-open-windows rule without telling him about the animals.

"We should close that window," she muttered, her heart beating fast.

"Then how are we going to run the power cords up into the clock?" Oliver asked, scratching his forehead again. "What's the big deal anyway? It's not like there are any bugs around here. I haven't even heard a cricket since we arrived."

Lucy frowned. No, there weren't any crickets, she thought.

But there *was* a crow.

EIGHT

WHO IS THE GARR?

While her brother washed off the remains of the acorn dust, Lucy peeked in on the animals in the broom closet. They were still there, tucked safely behind the box of lightbulbs where she'd left them. Lucy then ran up into the mechanical room and tried to shut the window. The window swung on a hinge like a ship's porthole and would not close completely with the power cord in the way.

Lucy groaned. The mechanical room door had been left open when Mr. Quigley showed up, so it was impossible to tell if the crow had flown inside and was hiding in another part of the house. Then again, the power cord had been dangling from the open window all night, so if the crow had wanted to get in, it could have done so at any time.

But the crow may not have known that Torsten and Meridian had come out of their hiding spot, Lucy told herself. And now that it did . . .

Lucy sighed. Here she was acting as if all these things were true when she still wasn't entirely sure she hadn't been dreaming. And was the crow really after the animals? Maybe it just looked that way. After all, birds flew into windows all the time in the city; why should it be any different out here in the boonies of Rhode Island? Still, Lucy thought it best to make sure the mechanical room door was always shut when her father and brother weren't working in there.

That way, if the crow got in, at least it would be trapped, and everyone would know about it.

All this weighed heavily on Lucy's mind in the kitchen during lunch, but when her father asked her what was wrong, Lucy decided to hold off telling him about the crow. It was too complicated to try to explain, and she already felt stupid enough for butting in about the clock earlier with Mr. Quigley.

"What does *sentient* mean?" she asked instead, and her father raised a curious eyebrow. "I came across it in one of the books in the library."

"Glad to see you're getting some summer reading done for once," said Mr. Tinker with a mouth full of tuna fish sandwich. "And *sentient* means something is able to feel or sense things."

"It can also mean something is alive," Oliver said irritably, scratching at his forehead and hands.

Lucy's heart began to beat very fast. Did Roger Blackford think his house was alive? But that was impossible. There had to be a perfectly logical explanation for why the painting over the hearth had turned black. Then again, if wooden animals could come alive here, then maybe the house itself could, too.

"What about *alchemy*?" Lucy asked, glancing around the kitchen uneasily, and her father and Oliver exchanged a look as if to say, *What the heck has this kid been reading?*

"Alchemy is just an old-fashioned name for chemistry, I think," said Mr. Tinker, polishing off the last of his sandwich. "You don't have to be Sherlock Holmes to conclude that a chemist used to live here, what with all that stuff in the library."

After lunch, Lucy searched the house for the crow while the others went back to work in the clock. Lucy was thankful that the doors to both the attic and the cellar were still dead-bolted from the outside. The attic was the creepiest room in the house, she thought. But, then again, she hadn't been down to the cellar yet.

Lucy began with the bedrooms upstairs, peeking under the beds, into the closets, and beneath the sheets that covered the furniture and even the paintings on the walls. Clearly, when Mr. Quigley bought the house, he bought *everything*, including the former residents' clothing, which still hung moth-eaten and mildewed in the armoires.

The last bedroom Lucy searched had once belonged to a little boy. Lucy knew this because, under the sheets, she found a rocking horse, a model train, some tin soldiers, a wooden drum, and other toys—all of them faded or rusty or falling apart, and much older than anything Lucy had ever seen in her father's shop.

However, there was something else: a gilded painting

that had fallen off the wall. Lucy had come across some other paintings upstairs during her search, but none like *this one*. It was on the floor, lying facedown on top of its sheet, as if both had fallen off the wall many years ago.

Lucy stood the painting upright against the wall, sending billows of dust across a shaft of sunlight that was streaming in through the window. The painting was a portrait of a young boy dressed in a black suit and a high-collared shirt. A blue sky and a rolling field with horses made up the background, but where the boy's face should have been, there was only a large, smoky black smudge.

The back of Lucy's neck prickled. The room had belonged to the Blackfords' son—the boy in the journal who had died, the infant Abigail Blackford had been holding in the painting above the fireplace until something turned it black. Oliver thought the painting had been damaged in a fire, but now Lucy knew better.

"'Our beloved son, Edgar,'" she read out loud from a brass plate at the bottom of the frame. "So that's your name," Lucy whispered. "Edgar Blackford. But what happened to you?"

Suddenly, the painting fell over with a *thud*!

Lucy shrieked and jumped back, nearly tumbled over the sheet-covered rocking horse, and then scrambled out into the hallway, where, for the briefest of moments, she thought she saw the wall sconces flicker red.

"Lucy, is that you?" her father called.

Heart pounding and breathless, Lucy ran over to the railing at the top of the stairs, where she found her father gazing up at her from the landing below. He was holding a wrench, and his face was all sweaty and covered in grease. He looked irritated.

"What are you doing? You look as if you've just seen a ghost."

"I—er—I was just exploring. I bumped into something and scared myself is all."

Lucy's father rolled his eyes and sighed. "Lucy, please. Everything in this house belongs to Mr. Quigley. You shouldn't be messing around with his stuff, you understand? What if you break something?"

"I'm sorry."

Lucy's father smiled and his eyes softened. "No, I'm the one who's sorry, kid. I know it must be a bit boring for you around here. Tell you what. Once Ollie and I get a handle on this pendulum, how about the three of us make a day of it at the beach? We haven't been since your mother—"

Lucy's father stopped and, swallowing hard, averted his eyes. Lucy understood. He didn't like talking about her mother—at least not with Lucy. Oliver's theory was, because they were so much alike, it was too painful. Lucy believed him. Oliver understood people in ways that Lucy didn't.

Mr. Tinker cleared his throat and began again. "Er— anyway—I'm sure Mr. Quigley won't mind if we have a little fun. Maybe in a couple of days? I need to run to the hardware store tomorrow for some parts. Your brother and I are going to build a custom winding mechanism."

Lucy smiled and nodded. A trip to the beach sounded wonderful, and all at once Lucy wasn't so scared anymore. She had let all that stuff about the house being sentient and burning the paintings get to her. *She* had knocked the painting over by accident. Lucy was sure of it now.

"Hey, Pop, the pendulum moved!" Oliver called, and Mr. Tinker disappeared inside the mechanical room. Lucy hurried down to the landing and stood in the doorway. Her father and brother were by the pendulum, examining it.

"Are you sure?" asked Mr. Tinker. "It looks in the same spot to me."

"I swear," Oliver said. "Right after Lucy shrieked, I saw it swing a whole foot out of the corner of my eye— Look!"

Mr. Tinker pushed hard on the pendulum arm. It wouldn't budge. "Well, it sure is stuck again now."

"I'm telling you, Pop, it moved. Maybe not a whole foot, but it moved!"

"All right," Mr. Tinker said with a sigh. "Slide that

ladder over here so I can have another look at that anchor and escape wheel."

As the others went back to work on the clock, Lucy bounded down the stairs and finished searching for the crow on the first floor. No sign of it anywhere. She checked on the animals in the broom closet again and then spent the rest of the afternoon in the library.

Lucy began with a closer read through the journal, and when she found nothing more about Edgar Blackford and the house being sentient, she moved on to the rest of the shelves. There were all sorts of books, most of which were about scientific things such as geology and plants and other stuff that Lucy thought was boring. Other books had titles that *sounded* interesting—*Great Expectations, The Count of Monte Cristo, War and Peace*—but the way they were written was too complicated and old-fashioned, so she just looked at the pictures. Soon, Lucy got bored with those, too, and turned her attention to the bottles and jars. Some had labels with chemical symbols and words that Lucy didn't understand, while others were either empty or had no labels at all.

Then Lucy came upon something called sunstone cream—which, according to the label on the jar, was for counteracting the effects of shadow wood. The jar was very dusty, and the contents were grayish and goopy and smelled even worse than the wood glue. Oliver had been complaining at lunch that his hands and forehead were still itching from the acorn. And so, later, over dinner, Lucy suggested that he try rubbing some of the sunstone cream on his skin. Her father quickly nixed the idea.

"Who knows how long that stuff has been lying around," he said, munching away on some canned ravioli that Oliver had heated up. "Besides, it's probably just snake oil. You couldn't trust medicine back then the way you can now."

Lucy didn't know what her father meant by snake oil, but he said that if Oliver's skin was still itchy in the morning, they would pick up some calamine lotion on their way back from the hardware store.

The Tinkers spent the rest of that second evening in Watch Hollow playing games again at the kitchen table. Tonight, however, it seemed to take *much longer*. Lucy wasn't nearly as scared of the shadows as she'd been the night before, but a couple of times her heart nearly stopped when she thought she saw the black shape of the crow fluttering among them. It was only her eyes playing tricks on her.

The family went to bed around ten o'clock, but Oliver took forever to fall asleep because his hands and forehead were so itchy. Lucy felt as if she might explode with anticipation when finally, just after eleven thirty according to

Oliver's watch on the nightstand, she heard him begin to snore.

Lucy, wearing only a sleeveless nightgown, slipped out of their bedroom and padded silently into the darkened kitchen, where she filled a bowl with tuna fish for Meridian and another with Spam for Torsten. Lucy had been planning this for hours and brought the bowls into the library, which was so bright with moonlight, she did not need a lantern to see. Lucy set the bowls on the hearth, quickly fetched Torsten and Meridian from the broom closet, and then set them on the hearth, too. She slid the library doors closed and then sat down in one of the chairs and waited. And waited.

"It *has* to be close to midnight now," Lucy muttered, glancing out one of the windows. The large swath of moonlit grass between the house and the Shadow Woods looked like a sea of rolling silver waves in the breeze. But when Lucy turned back to the animals, Meridian was gone.

Lucy gasped and tried to stand, but then something snatched her by her braid and yanked her back into the chair. Lucy shrieked and, despite her terror, realized dimly what had happened. Meridian had come alive and climbed up the back of her chair when Lucy wasn't looking. And now the cat was holding Lucy down with her claws to her throat.

"Never let your guard down, girl!" Meridian whispered in Lucy's ear.

Lucy squealed in panic and grabbed at Meridian's paws, but the cat, hissing loudly, pressed her claws deeper into Lucy's neck. Lucy winced at the pain.

"Careful or you'll cut yourself," Meridian droned.

"Meridian, no!" Torsten shouted, leaping up onto Lucy's lap.

"Shut up, Torsten!" Meridian snapped. "We have ourselves a prisoner now." She jerked Lucy violently in the chair. "Tell us, who is the Garr and how do we defeat him?"

"Miss Lucy doesn't serve the Garr!" Torsten cried. "She's the new caretaker. You saw how she protected us today!"

The Garr? Lucy wondered, heart pounding and mind racing. *Who is the Garr?*

Meridian chuckled menacingly. "You're too stupid for your own good, Torsten. This is a trick to have us lead her to the others. We are the house's last defense. This girl and her family are spies!"

Torsten frowned and wrinkled his brow. Clearly, he hadn't thought about that.

"We're not spies," Lucy said, breathless with fright. "And I've never heard of any Garr. I—I was just trying to help you!"

Meridian snickered. "You must think us idiots, girl.

Putting on your little caretaker act? You're good, I'll give you that. But you can't fool me. I will protect Blackford House until my dying breath!"

"Please!" Lucy said, on the verge of tears. "I swear, I don't know what's going on. Mr. Quigley hired my father to fix the clock!"

Meridian growled. "There's that name again. Quigley. Who is Mr. Quigley?"

"He owns the house now. He bought it a few months ago and hired my father to fix the clock. It generates the electricity—the clock, I mean—and, well, he won't move in until it's working."

"That makes sense, Meridian," Torsten said. "That man who was here before, he was working on the clock, too. Maybe this Mr. Quigley and the Tinkers are here to help restore the balance. Maybe the bad time is finally over!"

Lucy felt Meridian's grip relax.

"The house is weak, Torsten," the cat said. "All of us are weak. The balance is off, and the Garr will stop at nothing until the house is his. This is just another one of his tricks. He wants us to lead this girl to the others."

"I swear to you, I've never heard of this Garr," Lucy cried.

"What if she's telling the truth, Meridian?" Torsten asked. "What if Miss Lucy *is* the caretaker the house

106

has been waiting for all these years? And if she's not"—Torsten's stomach growled—"well, how much longer can we go on this way?"

A few tense seconds passed in which Lucy could feel Meridian's heart beating against her neck, and then the cat released her. Lucy exhaled with relief, and when she looked again, Meridian was by the hearth. That cat had moved quickly and without a sound. She jerked her muzzle at the bowls of food.

"Eat some," Meridian said, her eyes twinkling in the moonlight, and Lucy stared back at her, confused. "If it's safe for you, it's safe for us."

Lucy understood. She'd seen a movie once where this king always had a servant taste his food to make sure it wasn't poisoned. Lucy slipped onto the floor and stuffed some tuna fish and Spam into her mouth at the same time. It tasted awful, but she got it down, and in the next moment, Torsten and Meridian buried their faces in their bowls.

Lucy's heart twisted as she watched them eat. The animals were starving. Torsten lapped away obliviously at his Spam, while Meridian kept her eyes on Lucy the entire time she devoured her tuna. In less than a minute they were both finished.

"Boy, oh boy," Torsten said, licking his chops. "That was the best meal I've ever had. I can't thank you enough, Miss

Lucy. What do you say, Meridian? Would a servant of the Garr give us a meal like that?"

Meridian sat back on her hindquarters and licked her claws.

"We shall see," she said, her eyes narrowing. "We shall see."

"Who is the Garr?" Lucy asked.

"We don't know," Torsten said. "Tempus Crow was the first to utter his name."

"Tempus Crow? Is he the crow I saw today?"

Torsten bowed his head solemnly. "He was once wooden and part of the clock like us. But then he turned traitor and joined with the Garr, who made him a real crow. He is alive both day and night now."

"You expect us to believe you don't know this, girl?" Meridian asked.

Lucy nodded, and the cat sniffed cynically.

"Tempus Crow was the first to go," Torsten went on, ignoring her. "'*The Garr!*' we heard him cry on the night we came alive, and then he flew out of the clock and into the Shadow Woods. After that, the balance was lost. Tempus Crow was the cuckoo bird, after all. He cawed the time."

"So that's what you meant when you said you hadn't come alive until recently?"

"It's hard to explain, but we've always been alive up here,"

Torsten said, patting the top of his head. "In our natural state, our minds are at one with the clock. There is no sense of past or future, only the present, even though our bodies are wooden. It's quite pleasant, really. But then something happened—the arrival of the Garr, Meridian thinks—after which the clock stopped and we started coming alive in a different way after midnight. That's when Tempus Crow began snatching us and—"

"I don't understand. Why is Tempus Crow snatching you?"

"The Garr cannot enter the house. I've never seen him, but Meridian has, watching the house at night from the edge of the Shadow Woods. That's where he lives—a dark and twisted tree man, ten feet tall, with branches for arms and eyes like burning coals. He only comes out at night, though. Isn't that right, Meridian?"

The cat gulped and glanced nervously at the window. From Lucy's position on the floor, she could not see the Shadow Woods, but she imagined the creature Torsten had described standing amid the trees and watching the house as they spoke. Lucy shivered.

"Why can't the Garr enter the house?" she asked.

"The Garr is a creature of the Shadow Woods, and the Shadow Woods cannot get too close to the house either because of the stone here. Sunstone it's called."

"Sunstone"—Lucy pointed at the jars on the bookshelf—"you mean, the same stuff that cream is made from?"

"That's right," Torsten said. "The house is built from both shadow wood and sunstone. The Garr doesn't like sunstone. Tempus Crow, however, can come and go as he pleases because he was once part of the clock like us. And each time one of us disappears, the Shadow Woods get closer. It's only Meridian and myself and—"

Meridian hissed, and Torsten stopped himself. "Er—anyhow," the dog continued, "when we're gone, the house will belong to the Garr forever. At least, that's what Meridian thinks." Torsten turned to her. "Did I tell it right?"

"You've told too much, I think," Meridian said quietly. Lucy was about to ask who else was left in the house but then thought better of it. The cat was still very suspicious of her, and that was her biggest fear: that this Garr, whoever he was, was using Lucy to find the hiding spot—and whoever else was hiding there.

"Why would snatching you from the house affect the Shadow Woods?" Lucy asked instead. "I mean, what does one have to do with the other?"

"In the good times," Torsten said, "everything here worked in perfect harmony. Our places in the clock kept it ticking, and the Shadow Woods stayed put. The Shadow Woods doesn't like the light in the house. But then the clock stopped, the light went out, and the Shadow Woods began to creep closer."

"And yet, there is much more to this house than its clock," Meridian said. "*Everything* here was designed to work together in perfect balance—sunstone and shadow wood, light and dark, day and night. For in such balance there is potent magic."

"That's how we powered the clock," Torsten said. "Our eyes are made of sunstones, but our bodies are made of shadow wood. And even though the clock has stopped, our magic remains within these walls. Our magic is the only thing keeping the house alive."

Torsten's tongue lolled out of his mouth, and he smiled.

"So the house *is* sentient," Lucy muttered, and the animals regarded her quizzically. "I learned that word from reading Roger Blackford's journal." Lucy jerked her chin at it on the chemistry table. "Roger Blackford believed the house was alive."

"Oh, it is," said Torsten. "But not the way you are alive, Miss Lucy. Or even us, for that matter. The clock is the heart of the house, and even though the clock has stopped, because we animals are part of it, our magic, our presence here, is still too much for the Shadow Woods. We are hope, the only things keeping the house alive now—at least, before *you* arrived. After all, the caretaker is magical, too."

"Well, I'm sorry to disappoint you," Lucy said, "but there's nothing magical about me. I'm just a normal kid. Well . . . *mostly* normal."

"You're wrong," Torsten said. "There's magic in you, powerful magic that will get the clock ticking again. I just know it. You're the caretaker, after all, and the caretaker must be magical."

"I say we take the girl at her word," Meridian said sarcastically. "The clock is still broken, in case you haven't noticed."

"That's not her fault," Torsten protested. "The clock is probably weak, just like the rest of the house. None of us has dared go up there since Tempus Crow started snatching us but— Well, this Quigley fellow must be good, then. Same for the Tinkers if they're trying to fix the clock. What with most of us gone now, they would have to find a different way of powering it."

"Mr. Quigley fired the last clocksmith because he almost blew up the house," Lucy said. "The pendulum is the problem, he thinks, and my father and brother are going to build a winding mechanism to get it swinging again."

"There, you see, Meridian?" Torsten said. "These people don't serve the Garr. The Garr would never want the clock fixed. The clock—the clock is light. But most of all, the clock is balance. It keeps the Shadow Woods at bay, so maybe the bad time is over. Which means Lucy Tinker here *is* the caretaker."

Meridian, unconvinced, just rolled her eyes and sighed.

Lucy felt her cheeks go hot. Despite what Torsten thought, she *couldn't* be the caretaker. There was nothing magical about her, not to mention she didn't know the first thing about taking care of houses. She'd never even *lived* in one, and certainly had never imagined that such a place as Blackford House could ever exist outside of fairy tales. A magical house with a clock powered by wooden animals that generated light? A magical house that was built near, actually built *from*, a scary place called the Shadow Woods? And finally, a magical house with a creature named the Garr who wanted it for himself?

"The other animals must be starving, too," Lucy said suddenly. "You don't have to tell me where they're hiding, but we need to get them some food."

Torsten and Meridian looked at each other warily.

"Just tell me how much you need, and then you can bring it to them—"

At that moment, a low, cranking sound came from somewhere deep within the walls. The lights flickered bloodred, and then the faint but unmistakable sound of a clock ticking, slow and steady, began echoing through the house.

"The clock!" Torsten cried.

Lucy and the animals dashed from the library, through the parlor, and into the foyer, where the crystal chandelier was flashing. The ticking was louder out here, and Lucy gazed up at the clock. She could see light under the mechanical room door, and in the cracks between the cuckoo door, too.

"I told you, Meridian!" Torsten cried. "Miss Lucy is the new caretaker! Her magic has started the clock ticking again!"

"But the lights are *red*," Meridian muttered, glancing around.

And then the ticking of the clock was shattered by a scream.

NINE

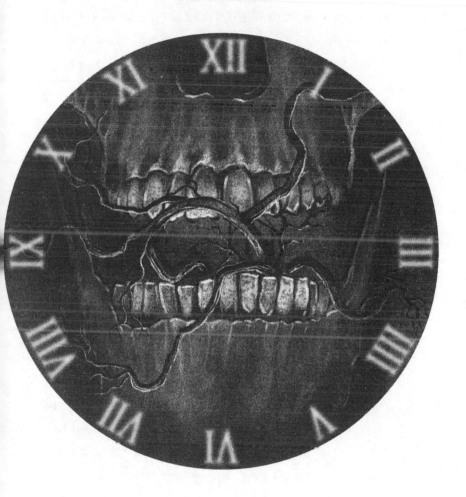

OLIVER'S HEAD, INSIDE AND OUT

*I*n his dream, Oliver was visiting his mother's grave. An enormous crow with acorns for eyes sat watching him from atop a headstone a few feet away.

"Good BOY—caw!" the crow said—throatily, and oddly stressing boy—and Oliver set down a bouquet of flowers in the overgrown grass.

"I miss you so much, Mom," Oliver whispered. He looked for the crow again, and instead spied his mother coming toward him among the headstones. She was dressed in a luminous white gown, and she looked healthy. Oliver's heart soared, and they embraced. His mother was soft and warm but smelled vaguely of leaves.

"I am very proud of you," she said, smiling down at him. Her eyes were radiant and yet far away, as if she were almost too tall for Oliver to see. "You are the man of the house now."

"You mean the house here in Watch Hollow?" Oliver asked, and his mother nodded.

"This is where we all belong," she said, and in the next moment, her face shriveled and turned black. Her eyes sank back into their sockets, and her skin flaked off in a whirlwind of ashes, revealing a grinning white skull underneath.

Oliver's lungs seized in horror. He tried to scream, but nothing came out.

Her black hair whipping in the wind, Oliver's mother

gripped him by the shoulders and bent down as if to kiss him. Oliver tried to turn away, but he could not move, he could not breathe as his mother's ghastly grin loomed closer. The jaw of her skull swung open, and a large, black acorn appeared between her teeth.

"This is where all of you belong!" she croaked, and then the acorn sprouted dozens of twisting black roots. They swarmed Oliver's face like tentacles, engulfing him in a teeming tangle of seamless black.

The air rushed into Oliver's lungs and he screamed. At the same time, the blackness dissolved into a different kind of blackness, one broken up with the shadows of a moonlit room and a crow perched on his chest. A crow?

"Boo!" the bird said, snapping open its beak, and Oliver gasped and bolted upright. It was only a dream, he understood on some level—he was back in his bed now at Blackford House—but somehow the crow was still there, fluttering up and away from him into the shadows!

Everything next happened in a blur. Oliver screamed again, the crow squeezed out through a sliver of open space at the bottom of the window, and then the casement slammed shut. At the same time, Lucy burst in through the doorway. She cried out her brother's name and rushed to his side. A moment later, their father appeared in the doorway, groggy and asking what happened.

"I—I—" Oliver sputtered, blinking around, "I had a nightmare and—"

Oliver shivered and burst into tears. Lucy hugged him, while their father flicked on the lantern and sat down on the opposite bed. Oliver was dimly aware of them trying to comfort him, but his mind was already trying to process what had happened. He'd never been so terrified. The nightmare about his mother had been so real—especially the part about the crow.

Oliver dragged the back of his hand across his nose and swiveled his eyes to the window. The crow, he thought, had been in his dream—and yet, he could still feel its weight and the imprint of its claws on his chest.

Oliver took a deep breath and pulled himself together. He suddenly felt ashamed, acting like such a wuss over a dream in front of his younger sister. But where had she been when he woke up? Oliver asked her, and in the dim lantern light, he thought Lucy looked almost guilty when she replied.

"Er—I was in the bathroom," she said hesitantly. "I heard you screaming and— Well, do you want to talk about it?"

Oliver shook his head. The last thing he wanted to do was upset everyone by telling them the details of his dream. Besides, it was already starting to grow fuzzy and dim inside his head.

"Funny," said Mr. Tinker, rubbing his eyes. "I was having the weirdest dream, too. Something about the clock being fixed. Matter of fact, when I woke up, I could've sworn I heard it ticking."

Oliver felt Lucy shift uncomfortably beside him—all this talk about bad dreams was scaring her, he thought—so he told the others that he wanted to go back to bed. Mr. Tinker wished the children goodnight and returned to his bedroom, while Lucy grabbed her pillow and slid under the covers with her brother—head to toe, just as they always slept in their bed back home. Neither of them said a word, and for a long time, Oliver lay there in the moonlight, trying to ignore the fragments of his dream that still haunted him.

Eventually, Oliver fell asleep. There were no more dreams, only a long, black blink, and when next he opened his eyes, the room was gray with the soft light of dawn. And there was Lucy, sleeping soundly at the foot of his bed.

Oliver's heart twisted. What a jerk he was for scaring her. And come to think of it, had the dream really been *that* scary? It was all a murky jumble now in his head—the graveyard, his mother, something about a skull and a crow. And there was something else, too; something that his mother had said—or given him, maybe—but for the life of him, Oliver couldn't remember.

Oliver grabbed his glasses from the nightstand and slipped silently into the bathroom across the hall. The smell of coffee drifted in from the kitchen, which meant his father was awake, too. He'd set up one of the library's antique oil burners on the stove the night before so they wouldn't have to use the generator just to boil water.

The light filtering in through the tiny window above the tub was barely enough to see anything, which is why, when Oliver caught sight of his reflection in the bathroom mirror, he thought at first that his eyes were playing tricks on him. Oliver blinked and touched his forehead. His eyes might be lying but his fingers weren't.

The pimples on his forehead were completely gone.

Oliver's mouth hung open. His chin was still a mess, but—

A lightbulb went on in his head. The acorn dust in his pocket. He'd only touched his forehead with it.

Oliver quickly washed and dressed and hurried out into the kitchen, where he joined his father at the table and poured them each a bowl of cereal. Oliver waited for his father to notice his skin, but when he didn't, Oliver pointed out his forehead and explained his theory about the acorn dust. His father chuckled.

"Probably just a coincidence," he said. "But if not, you've got a great career ahead of you as a dermatologist."

Oliver was so excited that he completely forgot about his dream and spent the next hour or so with his father in the clock, taking measurements for the new winding mechanism. They had decided that the best place for it would be on the floor between the pipe coupling for the *six* hole and the iron sphere in the center of the machinery—the conductor sphere, Mr. Tinker called it.

"A winding mechanism attached to the conductor sphere will jump start the pendulum," he said, shinnying on his back under some gears. "The conductor sphere distributes the shadow wood energy to the rest of the clock."

Then why did the other clocksmith try to reroute pipes back into the clock face? Oliver wondered. He stood on his tippy-toes and stuck his fingers into the pipe coupling for the *three* hole—which on the other side, Oliver remembered, was shaped like a rabbit.

"Do you think Mr. Quigley might be wrong about the missing statues being decorative?" Oliver asked, and his father squirted some oil into the gears.

"What do you mean?"

"Well, if shadow wood powers the clock, maybe the pipes used to connect to the missing statues. Maybe they were made of shadow wood, and, you know, they worked like batteries or something. You think maybe the other guy was just trying to put the pipes back where they belonged?"

"I doubt that, Ollie. Mr. Quigley said the previous clock-smith nearly blew up the house. Besides, the couplings are just bolted into the stone—the holes don't go all the way through. Maybe that was the other fella's intention—you know, to drill some holes and carve new statues at some point. But with an entire wall of shadow wood, I don't see why he'd need to do that. . . ."

Mr. Tinker trailed off, his attention on oiling the gears, and Oliver examined the coupling on the back of the *eight* hole—the one for the pig. The coupling appeared to be older than the couplings in the wall of shadow wood, but that didn't mean the clock wasn't in its present configuration when the previous clocksmith started working on it—which would make sense if the statues had been missing for some time and the clock had been reconfigured to run off the shadow wood.

Oliver stuck his finger into the pig coupling and felt the cold brick inside. Maybe his father was right. Since the pipes didn't go through to the animal holes, even if the statues had been made from shadow wood, they couldn't have acted as batteries—which meant they really were just decorative after all. In addition to the cat, pig, rabbit, rat, duck, dog, and turtle, Oliver had discovered the other holes had once housed a beaver, a squirrel, a raccoon, a skunk, and a fawn—all animals one might find in the woods surrounding the property, his father pointed out. But what that had to do with anything, Oliver had no idea.

Oliver impulsively moved to the round window on the back wall and gazed out at the woods. He hadn't seen so much as a fly since they'd arrived, never mind rabbits and deer. But who could blame them? *If I were an animal,* Oliver thought, *I wouldn't want to live in the Shadow Woods either.*

Then again, the Shadow Woods couldn't be *all* bad. Teddy and his father lived in them—not to mention, the Shadow Woods were filled with acne-curing acorns. Oliver touched his forehead. He still couldn't get over how it had cleared up. Maybe there was some truth in what Teddy said; maybe the Shadow Woods *were* magical after all!

Clang! The sound of his father dropping a wrench startled Oliver from his thoughts, and he turned around to find him on his back with his face covered in oil. Oliver burst out laughing.

"Yeah, yeah, very funny," his father grumbled, wiping off the oil with a rag, and then he glanced at his watch. "It's almost eight. Why don't you make yourself useful and load those empty gas cans onto the truck—we can fill up on the way back from the hardware store. And wake Lucy, too, while you're at it. If she ever wants to get to the beach, she'll have to start pulling her weight around here. . . ."

Mr. Tinker trailed off again as he cleaned up the oil, and

in a flash, Oliver bounded outside and headed straight for the carriage house. He was so preoccupied that he didn't notice how much the Shadow Woods had advanced until he'd stepped into them.

Oliver froze at the entrance to the carriage house, which was now completely covered in branches. And not only that, there were trees growing *in front* of it, too—just a half dozen or so saplings that were not there the day before, and that couldn't have possibly grown so quickly overnight.

"Quite remarkable, isn't it?" someone said, and Oliver whirled to find Teddy standing at the entrance to the tunnel in the woods twenty or so yards away. He was dressed in the same old-fashioned hunting outfit and cap and, in one outstretched palm, held something round and black. Oliver's heart began to pound. Even from a distance, he could tell what it was.

An acorn.

As Oliver hurried over, he noticed that the flagstone path seemed shorter—which meant the Shadow Woods had advanced here, too. Then again, Oliver couldn't be sure. The trees at the entrance to the tunnel were older than the trees by the carriage house, and the flagstones still ended at the edge of the woods as they did the day before. However, something about the path there looked different, Oliver realized as he drew closer; it was as if the flagstones had been removed and the dirt freshly tamped at Teddy's feet.

"Don't be alarmed," Teddy said, rolling the acorn between his thumb and forefinger. "That is one of the peculiarities of the Shadow Woods. When they expand, they do so very fast. You arrived at the height of the growing season. I imagine, however, all that's nearly done. Mr. Quigley told my father that he plans on trimming back the trees after he moves in. Better hop to it soon, don't you think?"

Teddy chuckled, and Oliver swallowed hard. "Speaking of your *fa*-ther," he said, his voice cracking again, "I was wondering if I could ask him a couple of questions."

Teddy's eyes darkened. "Why would you want to do that?"

"It's just that, well, Mr. Quigley told us your father tried something different with the clock, and I wanted to ask him—you know—if he might have any advice for us."

Teddy seemed to consider this for a moment.

"The trick is to get that pendulum moving," he said finally. "My father explained to me that, the way the clock works in conjunction with the properties of the shadow wood, everything is cyclical and self-perpetuating."

Oliver blinked back at Teddy blankly.

"Simply put, once you get the pendulum moving, the shadow wood will keep it moving forever. You're the son of a clocksmith. Don't tell me you've never heard of a perpetual motion clock?"

"Oh—yes, of course," Oliver said. "A perpetual motion clock doesn't need to be wound. It runs on temperature and atmospheric pressure changes—you know, the expansion and contraction of gases—that are contained in airtight bellows. The bellows are connected to the clock's mainspring, so when the gases expand and contract, the bellows move the mainspring and it doesn't have to be *wound*."

Oliver cleared his throat—stupid voice cracking—and Teddy smiled.

"Impressive," he said. "Perhaps Mr. Quigley should've hired *you*."

"But the clock here can't be a perpetual motion clock," Oliver said, more to himself. "It doesn't have any bellows or the right kind of mainspring."

"The way I understand it, the shadow wood provides the temperature and atmospheric changes. In a manner of speaking, that is."

"Yeah, but the pendulum mechanism is all wrong for a perpetual motion clock. Then again, there are those pipes—and clearly the iron sphere in the middle is a conductor for the magnetic energy—"

"Precisely," Teddy said. "When the pendulum moves, the energy from the shadow wood in the house flows through the pipes. And when the energy from the shadow wood flows through the pipes, the pendulum moves. Perpetually."

"So, did your father think a new winding mechanism was the answer?"

Teddy shrugged. "My father was an amateur compared to yours. But again, the way I understand it, all the pendulum needs is a powerful enough kick start—either manually or from a burst of shadow wood energy through the pipes. Unfortunately, the stones there in the house and around the property counteract the energy of the shadow wood. A type of granite that the locals call sunstone. Nasty stuff, really. Consequently, you need a powerful enough burst of shadow wood energy to neutralize it. Perhaps even just one more might do the trick."

"Your father tried to reroute the pipes into the clock face, didn't he?" Oliver said, the light dawning. "That's why he almost blew up the house—the bricks in the clock face are made of sunstone!"

Teddy frowned and, without warning, tossed the acorn onto one of the flagstones at Oliver's feet. The acorn smoked and sizzled, flared briefly, and then crumbled into ash. Oliver's mouth hung open in disbelief.

"Sunstone and shadow wood are dangerous together," Teddy said. "Unfortunately for my father, he learned this lesson the hard way. The shadow wood in the house is much stronger than that poor acorn there, but still the sun-stone has a negative effect on it. You just get that pendulum moving with the shadow wood energy and all will be well."

Oliver, still stunned from the reaction of the acorn and the flagstone—which was *sunstone*, he now realized—swallowed hard and made to speak. His voice cracked, so he swallowed again.

"But how come the shadow wood energy never runs out?" Oliver asked. "I mean, there is no such thing as a *true* per-petual motion clock—that is, a clock that runs forever. Even the most advanced of them has to be recharged eventually."

Teddy smiled and produced another acorn from his pocket.

"As you yourself said, it really is all about the atmosphere in the house. The Shadow Woods work in ways that very few people understand. But isn't that the way of things? There is great power in the unknown."

Oliver blinked back at Teddy, confused, and Teddy pointed to Oliver's forehead.

"The outside of your head has already discovered the Shadow Woods' power. Now the inside needs to catch up." He held out the acorn for Oliver. "Go ahead, take it."

Oliver took the acorn, brushing Teddy's palm with his fingertips. Teddy's skin was ice cold.

"There are very few acorns this time of year," Teddy

said, looking around. "The trees don't start dropping them until mid-September. However, if I run across any, I can bring them to you, if you'd like."

Oliver's stomach squeezed excitedly—his zits were as good as gone forever!

"Sure, that'd be great," Oliver said, pushing up his glasses, and then his voice cracked on "*Thanks.*"

"No, thank *you,*" Teddy said, smiling. "It's nice to have someone my age around here for a change, even if it's just for a few weeks. It can get a little lonely living in the woods. Maybe when your work is done, you can come play with me sometime. Or we can go fishing."

Oliver's eyes flitted up at the trees. Just the idea of playing in the Shadow Woods made him nervous; imagine what Teddy must feel like *living* in them.

"Er—yeah—or we can hang here," Oliver said, jerking his thumb back at the house.

Teddy's smile faltered, and his eyes flickered with alarm.

"Mr. Quigley won't allow it," he said tersely. "Given that my father nearly blew up the old man's house, I think you can understand why."

"That's too bad," Oliver said. "But hey, at least he's allowing you guys to stay on in the caretaker's cottage, right? How long have you been living there?"

Teddy's face grew sad. "Much too long," he said, and a

breeze moaned through the tunnel, rustling the leaves and rattling the branches behind him. Oliver caught a whiff of something foul and garbagy.

"I need to go," Teddy said quietly. "If I find any more acorns, I'll bring them to you. They turn into powder when you bring them inside the house—the effect of the sunstone, of course—but their medicinal properties remain. Just don't let your acorns *touch* the sunstone. The poor things are not strong enough yet for that."

Teddy pointed to the flagstone at Oliver's feet. There was no sign anywhere of the acorn he'd tossed. Oliver nodded numbly. Teddy turned and walked slowly into the woods, his shape getting darker and darker until he dissolved into the shadows.

Oliver ran toward the house, his eyes never leaving his acorn, and as soon as he reached the back door, the acorn began to shrivel and grow warm in his hand. Oliver's heart pounded with excitement, and by the time he entered the kitchen, the acorn had turned to dust and his hand was itching.

Without thinking, Oliver rubbed the acorn dust on his chin and then, for good measure, all over his face, which began to itch at once. Oliver forced himself to endure it so that, as Teddy said, the medicinal properties could take effect. Soon, however, the itching turned to burning, and

Oliver raced into the bathroom and washed his hands and face. The burning stopped, but the itching was worse than ever. *Still, a small price to pay for no more zits*, he thought.

Oliver darted across the hall and poked his head into the bedroom he shared with Lucy. She was still asleep upside down in his bed.

"Come on, Lucy, wake *up!*" he shouted, his voice cracking, and with a gasp, Lucy bolted upright.

"The animals!" she cried, looking around, and Oliver knocked on the dresser beside the door.

"Hey, you're still dreaming. Come on, we've got a bunch of errands to run!"

Lucy nodded groggily and rubbed the sand from her eyes, and then Oliver ran back outside and into the carriage house—he'd almost forgotten about the gas cans. There were six, so it took him three trips back and forth to load them onto the truck.

When he was finished, Oliver stood for a moment gazing out at the Shadow Woods at the bottom of the driveway. He couldn't tell if the trees there were any closer, but all that didn't seem to matter anymore. At least not now, with the sun shining and his cheeks hurting—not from the acorn dust, he realized, but because he couldn't stop smiling.

TEN

THE CARETAKER

The second longest day of Lucy Tinker's life began and ended with the same thought:

The animals!

Lucy awoke worried sick about them. Had Torsten and Meridian waited all night for her to return with the food? Did they make it back to their hiding spot before dawn—and before Tempus Crow had a chance to snatch them? Lucy shivered.

"Some caretaker I am," she muttered, slipping on a T-shirt. She could just kick herself for being so stupid. Her plan had been to return with more food after Oliver fell asleep, but incredibly, Lucy fell asleep first! And look at the time—8:09 according to her brother's watch on the nightstand. The animals were already wooden again!

Lucy threw on a pair of shorts and hurried barefoot through the house and into the library. Torsten and Meridian were nowhere to be found, but Lucy noticed the box of Froot Loops she'd thrown away the day before was missing from the wastebasket. She remembered seeing it just before the animals came alive at midnight, so Lucy figured that they must have taken the cereal back to their hiding spot.

"Sorry I didn't bring more food," she shouted, hoping the animals could hear her. "I waited for Oliver to fall asleep, but I fell asleep first."

Lucy slumped into the big leather armchair and looked around. It was another beautiful day, but it was still early, so her windows didn't look as magical as they would later on, when the sunlight hit them just right.

Funny. When Lucy first saw her windows, she had wished the house was magical. But now that she knew it was, Lucy sort of wished it wasn't. It was a huge responsibility being the caretaker of a normal house, never mind a magical one—even if it was just for the summer.

Lucy closed her eyes and sank deeper into the chair. She was exhausted, and her thoughts were all muddy—not to mention she could still hear the clock ticking in her head. The clock was the answer, but the Garr was the problem. The clock was good, the clock was light, Torsten had said. But the Garr, a ten-foot-tall tree man who lived in the Shadow Woods, hated the clock and wanted the house for himself.

Lucy opened her eyes and gazed out the window. The Garr lived in the Shadow Woods, yes, but Blackford House was *built* from shadow wood. So was the clock—or at least, so were the animals that used to power it. And if Torsten was right and it had been Lucy's magic that had started the clock ticking again last night, then maybe the shadow wood in the house absorbed the goodness of the people who lived here—which meant the Shadow Woods couldn't be *all* bad.

This was Lucy's theory anyway, and one that she had come up with while she was lying awake the night before. The clock, she realized, had started ticking when she was trying to do good, when she was trying to *take care of* the animals. If only her brother hadn't had that nightmare and distracted her. Poor guy. Lucy had never heard him scream like that, but still, talk about bad timing.

Either way, one thing was certain: once the clock was fixed, things would be better for *everyone*. The light would return, and the Garr would go away. The animals would be safe, her father would get his money, and Mr. Quigley could move into the house and become its caretaker.

Did Mr. Quigley know the house was magical? The way he was acting yesterday, he must know *something* is up. But the animals didn't know who he was, which meant he probably didn't know about them either. And then there was Lucy's father.

Lucy decided not to tell him the truth just yet. He wouldn't believe her anyway. Parents never believed their kids when it came to things like talking animals and monsters in the woods. And in the movies, when grown-ups got involved in anything magical, they either messed things up or tried to make money off the situation.

Oliver, on the other hand, *might* believe her. But Lucy thought it best not to tell him anything until she got permission from Meridian. Lucy needed the cat's trust if she was going to help the animals. Things might even work out better if she kept her mouth shut. Her father would fix the pendulum and then Lucy would get the clock ticking with all the good deeds she did for the animals. She *was* their caretaker, after all.

Just then the soles of her feet began to itch. Lucy scratched at them, and scraped off some black dust that had clotted between her toes. Lucy sniffed her fingers.

"Oh no," Lucy moaned. It was the acorn dust. She recognized the smell, like burning leaves, from when she'd helped Oliver wash the dust off his face the day before. She must have stepped in it somewhere. And now her fingers were itching, too.

Lucy quickly retraced her steps back through the house and into the kitchen, where she found a small patch of dust on the floor near the door to the servants' hallway. There were also some smudgy footprints leading away from it. Lucy quickly washed her feet at the sink with a dish towel and then wiped up the dust from the floor. Her feet and her fingers were driving her crazy now, and the thought of having to wait to get some calamine lotion made her feel even crazier.

"Sunstone cream," Lucy muttered, remembering the jar from the day before, and she hurried back into the library.

Lucy pulled the jar from the bookshelf and read the label aloud. "'For counteracting the effects of shadow wood,'" she whispered, and unscrewed the lid. The grayish goop smelled even worse than she remembered, but Lucy rubbed some of it on her feet anyway, and the itching stopped at once. Lucy sighed with relief, and in the next moment heard her father's truck sputtering to a start out front.

Honk, honk, honk!

Lucy returned the jar to the bookshelf, quickly grabbed her flip-flops from the foyer, and joined the others in the truck. As soon as Lucy slid into the backseat, Oliver held his nose and winced. Lucy's cheeks grew hot.

"Yeah, well, if someone didn't spill acorn dust on the floor for me to step in, I wouldn't have had to use that sunstone cream to stop my feet from itching!"

There was a brief round of arguing. Lucy's father reprimanded her for messing with "snake oil," and Oliver defended his use of the acorn dust. Even Lucy had to admit his forehead looked amazing. Oliver then explained how that Teddy kid had given him another acorn this morning and that it had turned to dust when he'd entered the house.

Lucy wondered if Teddy and his father knew anything about the Garr. They *lived* in the Shadow Woods, after all— which meant maybe Meridian could be mistaken and there was no Garr, just that traitor Tempus Crow. Either way, before Lucy could think of a way to ask Oliver about it, her father said: "Maybe I should speak to Mr. Quigley about getting some scientists over here to check things out. Who knows? There might be some money in this for all of us."

Lucy pressed her lips together tightly. This was exactly why you couldn't tell grown-ups about things like magic and stuff. They always wanted to make a buck off it.

As the truck sputtered down the driveway and into the woods, the conversation between Oliver and her father got a little too technical for Lucy's taste—something about perpetual motion and the atmosphere and the right kind of mainspring—and by the time they crossed the stone bridge at the rocky stream, she had completely tuned them out.

Lucy closed her eyes and laid back her head. The wind felt good on her face, and for the next twenty minutes or so, she drifted in and out of sleep as her father and Oliver continued to talk about the clock—their voices disjointed at times and far away. Every now and then Lucy's eyes would flutter open to the trees or a farm or a low fieldstone wall rushing by. But then Oliver said something that *really* caught her attention.

"Mr. Quigley can't expect us to build one of those, too. Heck, I doubt he could find *anyone* who makes cuckoo birds that big."

Lucy's eyes snapped open, and she sat up straight. The

cuckoo bird—Tempus Crow—she'd forgotten to make sure the mechanical room door was closed!

Lucy's heart began to hammer as she scrambled for an excuse to turn back. Her mind was a blank, and before she knew it, they had reached civilization and her father swung the truck into a Home Depot parking lot. Lucy groaned in frustration. There was no way her father would turn back now. What was she going to do?

The next few hours were excruciating. The trip to Home Depot wasn't too bad, but then her father and brother dragged Lucy to an old junkyard, where they took forever looking for parts for the custom winding mechanism. After that, the Tinkers headed toward the coast for some clam cakes. Lucy was so on edge that she barely ate, but neither her father nor Oliver noticed. They were too busy talking about the clock—not to mention, Oliver had his own problems. His face had broken out into a rash and was itchier than ever.

"What did I tell you about messing with snake oil?" Mr. Tinker said with a mouth full of clam cake. Oliver tried to suck it up, refusing his father's offer to pick up some calamine lotion. But after a quick visit to the supermarket and a stop to fill up the gas cans, Oliver couldn't take it anymore and they swung by the drugstore. Oliver started applying the calamine lotion as soon as he was out the door, and by the time the Tinkers arrived back at the house, Lucy thought his face looked like a pink frosted cupcake.

Lucy bounded out of the truck, into the house, and up the stairs to the clock, where she found the mechanical room door closed. Lucy nearly collapsed with relief. She'd been worrying all day for nothing.

While her father and brother unloaded the truck, Lucy put away the groceries, making sure to set some aside for the animals. Then she began tidying up the library. Her plan was to leave some food by the fireplace after the others went to bed. The fireplace seemed the most likely place for the hiding spot because that was the direction from which the animals appeared to be coming when she'd first found them. Lucy had just finished sweeping the hearth when Oliver appeared in the library doorway.

"I think I used too much *a*-corn dust," he said, voice cracking. He sounded on the verge of tears. "The calamine lotion isn't working."

Lucy smiled, and without a word, retrieved the jar of sunstone cream from the bookshelf and rubbed it all over Oliver's face—*twice*. The first time was there in the library; the second, later that evening, just before Oliver got into bed.

His itching cured, Oliver fell asleep quickly. A short time later, Lucy heard their father snoring in his room.

Lucy stuffed her pillow under her sheets to make it look like her body just in case Oliver woke up—that's how prisoners in the movies always tricked the guards when they escaped. Then she hurried out into the kitchen and began preparing the animals' food, which consisted of more tuna and Spam, as well as some beef stew and a half loaf of white bread.

Lucy wasn't sure how many animals were in hiding, so she set out six bowls and a plate for the bread in a bright spot of moonlight near the fireplace in the library. Lucy had also worn Oliver's watch just to be safe, and at precisely five minutes till midnight, she announced:

"I've brought you some food. I hope it's enough, but if not, I'll be in the parlor so I don't see your hiding spot. Just let me know if you need more."

Lucy cocked her ear, hoping that this act of caretaking might start the clock ticking again; but when nothing happened, she slipped out of the library, slid the doors closed, and sat down in the parlor. A shaft of moonlight was hitting the painting above the hearth in such a way that Roger and Abigail Blackford looked like zombies, and the black smudge in Abigail's arms looked like a tiny ghost. Lucy's skin crawled.

Our beloved son, Edgar . . .

Lucy dropped her eyes to her brother's watch—11:57,

11:58, 11:59—12:00! Lucy sat forward in her chair and listened, and a moment later heard what sounded like one of the bowls scraping against the hearth in the library. The animals!

Lucy padded over to the library and pressed her ear against the doors. Munching sounds, and an *oink-oink* coming from the other side. One of the animals must be the pig that went in the clock's *eight* hole. Lucy tapped on the door gently.

"It's me, Lucy," she said. "Do you need me to bring you more food?"

A moment of tense silence, and then some whispering and another *oink-oink*.

"But she can help Fennish!" Torsten said—Lucy recognized his voice—but who was Fennish?

More whispering, some rustling and the clank of dishes on the hearth, and then Meridian said, "Come in."

Lucy slipped into the library and closed the doors behind her. The cat was sitting atop the chemistry table.

"We need your help," she said, nodding at the hearth, and Lucy spied four animals. In addition to Torsten, there was a pig, a rabbit, and a large rat lying on its side in the shadows. One of its eyes was closed, and over the other was a leather patch. The poor thing was wheezing and breathing rapidly.

"We found him in the parlor last night after you went

to bed," Torsten said. "Tempus Crow snatched him over a week ago. He must have escaped and made it back into the house through one of the secret passageways—"

"Fear . . . fear sows the seed . . . ," the rat moaned.

"He's delirious," Meridian said. "Was going on like that last night, too."

Lucy knelt and placed her hand on Fennish's side. She could feel the rat's heartbeat, but his breathing was shallow, and there were three long, blood-caked gashes running parallel to his emaciated rib cage.

"Please, miss, do something!" the rabbit whined, and the pig cried: "You're the caretaker, aren't you—*oink-oink!*"

"Quiet, you two, and let her think," Torsten said, and Lucy leaped to her feet.

"I'll be right back," she said, hurrying out. Lucy closed the doors behind her and dashed through the house into the kitchen. She slung a dish towel over her shoulder and filled her father's coffeepot with water. She also grabbed the rack and burner he'd been using on the stove, a book of matches, and a small battery-powered lantern, and then carried everything back into the library, where again she closed the doors.

The animals watched her closely, their eyes wide and twinkling as Lucy lit the burner and set the pot of water to boil on the metal rack above it. Then she knelt beside

Fennish and examined him more closely in the light from the lantern. His grizzled muzzle was caked with blood, and his wounds resembled claw marks. The rat was panting harder now, and on his breath Lucy caught a whiff of burning leaves. It was a scent that reminded her of—

"The acorn," Lucy muttered, her eyes landing on the jar of sunstone cream on the table. Tempus Crow had taken Fennish into the Shadow Woods, and sunstone cream was good for *counteracting* the effects of shadow wood. Maybe, just maybe . . .

A moment later, the water began to boil. Lucy soaked the rag in it and cleaned Fennish's wounds. Then she gently applied the sunstone cream. The rat twitched and moaned, and then suddenly, his wounds began to sparkle and glow.

Everyone gasped, and in the next moment, the sparkles dissolved and Fennish's side was completely healed.

"Thank you," he croaked, peering at Lucy through one half-open eye, and then the rat passed out.

Meridian rushed over to him and pressed her ear against his side. "He's exhausted. But his breathing is normal and his heartbeat steady. He will live."

Lucy sat back and let out a breath she hadn't realized she'd been holding.

"You did it!" Torsten exclaimed, hopping into her lap and licking her cheeks. "Nessie—Reginald—what'd I tell you? Miss Lucy is the caretaker!"

"Hooray for Miss Lucy!" the rabbit and the pig cheered, jumping around.

"Leave it to lucky number seven to escape the Garr," Meridian said, gazing down at the rat fondly. "Rest well, old friend, and then you shall eat." Meridian turned to Lucy. "You have done well. Thank you."

"Yes, thank you!" said the pig. "My name is Reginald Eight, by the way—*oink!*"

"And I'm Nessie Three," said the rabbit, wiggling her ears. "Thank you, thank you, Miss Lucy!"

"You're welcome," Lucy said. "But Meridian is right. Fennish will need to eat something—but only a little at a time at first until he gets his strength back. That's the way Mom had to eat when—"

Lucy's heart squeezed. She'd been so caught up in things over the last couple of days, she'd hardly thought about her mother at all. The animals blinked back at her expectantly, and Lucy forced a smile.

"Er—anyway," she said. "How did Tempus Crow snatch him?"

"Fennish was the one who brought us food after we went into hiding," Torsten said. "Being a rat, he knew how to use the secret passages better than any of us."

"The house showed us the hiding spot and other

passages after the clock stopped," Meridian said. "As if it knew what was coming and wanted to protect us."

"But still, it couldn't save Fennish—*oink!* The house tried, but that old clocksmith blocked his way, and Tempus Crow snatched him—*oink-oink!*"

"Is that how Fennish lost his eye?"

"Oh no," Torsten said. "Little Eddie did that to him years ago."

"Little Eddie? You mean Edgar Blackford?" The animals shifted uncomfortably. "I read about him in Roger Blackford's journal. He was the son of the people who built this place, right? There's a painting of him upstairs—it's burned all black and smudgy—like the painting of the Blackfords in the parlor."

"The paintings have been like that ever since he died," Nessie said. "Eddie was *not* a very nice boy, after all."

"What happened to him?"

"There are places in this world where magic is real," Meridian said, her eyes twinkling. "Places where the water, the plants, the earth, even the air is enchanted. Watch Hollow is one of those places. The Blackfords settled here over a century ago because they understood how to use the magic in the sunstone and shadow wood together in perfect balance. We are an example of that balance."

"Because your eyes are made of sunstone," Lucy said,

"but your bodies are shadow wood. It's the magical balance of the two that brings you to life."

"Right, but Eddie was *im*-balanced—*oink!*" said Reginald. "And for some reason, he couldn't bear the sight of Fennish Seven whenever he walked past the clock. And so, out of spite, he gouged out one of his eyes. The Blackfords punished him for what he did, but Eddie was so angry that he ran off into the Shadow Woods—*oink-oink!*"

"It was then that something happened," said Meridian. "Edgar tried to use the magic in the Shadow Woods to exact his revenge. However, because he was not an alchemist yet like his parents, his plan backfired, and the boy perished. The paintings have been like that ever since."

Lucy's heart pounded with excitement. "His parents were alchemists?" she asked, and Meridian nodded at the table. "Like chemists, you mean?"

"Sort of. Alchemy is actually a magical form of chemistry. The goal of alchemy is to purify and perfect the world around us. Alchemists can turn lead into gold and have long searched for the secret of immortality—"

"That's why the Blackfords built the clock—*oink!*" Reginald interjected. "They wanted to make themselves immortal. Obviously, they failed at that—*oink-oink!*"

"However," Meridian went on, "the clock breathed life into the house, which is how it maintained itself for decades at the same time it kept the Shadow Woods at bay—all the while we waited for the new caretaker to arrive."

"And now you're here!" Torsten said, tongue lolling and tail wagging.

"Well, I'm only here for the summer," Lucy said. "But I'll do what I can to protect you before Mr. Quigley takes over. He'll be the caretaker once the clock is fixed."

"Speaking of which," Meridian said. "Do you know why the lights were red last night when the clock started ticking? And do you know why the clock stopped?"

Lucy shook her head and sighed. "I don't know anything about the lights. And I'm afraid I don't know much about the clock either. I thought maybe Oliver distracted me with his nightmare. You know, because maybe my caretaking was what got the clock ticking again."

"Of course it was!" Torsten said. "You are the new caretaker, so you are magical just like we are. We can't power the clock without Tempus Crow and the rest of the animals. So, whatever those clocksmiths are doing, it's obviously working. The clock is somehow feeding off your magic."

Lucy looked over her shoulder. The library doors were closed, but still, if the clock had started ticking again, she'd be able to hear it—not to mention the lights would be on. Maybe she was wrong. Maybe her caretaking *wasn't* what got the clock ticking. After all, wouldn't her most recent act of kindness toward Fennish have affected it? Unless the pendulum was damaged worse than she thought. Her father and Oliver were banging around up there for a long time after supper.

"Anyway," Lucy went on, "the clock is my father and brother's specialty. I'm not sure how Pop would react if he knew the truth about this place, but Oliver would be cool. He's really into comics and . . . well, weird stuff like this always happens in comics. Plus, I know he'd want to help. He's the best, really. Maybe if you told him what you told me, he can figure out a way to get the clock ticking for good."

The animals regarded one another nervously.

"Clearly, the house does not want us to reveal ourselves to outsiders," Meridian said. "That's why it showed us the hiding spot—to keep us out of sight and protect us."

"That's right—*oink!*" Reginald said. "Fennish Seven revealed himself last time by accident, when he was stealing the clocksmith's food. That old man tried to kill him with a hammer—*oink!* The house defended him as best it could, then Tempus Crow snatched him. The clocksmith fled soon after that—*oink-oink!*"

Nessie the rabbit groaned anxiously. "Can you imagine what would happen should the wrong person learn of our existence?"

"And then there's the house itself," Meridian said.

"There is powerful magic here when that clock is working, and should the wrong person get their hands on it—"

"But Oliver is *not* the wrong person—"

"He's not the caretaker; *you* are," Meridian said. "And so, it is your duty not only to protect us, but also to obey the house's wishes."

"I'm sorry, Lucy," Torsten said. "Meridian's right. That's why I went wooden that first night. I knew you were the caretaker the moment you fixed my ear. But your brother— well, he might be a nice boy, but he's not the caretaker."

Lucy frowned and bit her lip. How was she going to keep all this secret for the whole summer?

"Besides," Torsten said, "you already knew this deep down, didn't you? I mean, you haven't told your brother yet, or your father, have you? That proves beyond a shadow of a doubt that you're the caretaker. Only the caretaker would know in her heart to protect the magic that lives on here."

Lucy sighed. Her earlier reasoning for keeping things secret from Oliver and her father seemed stupid now. She was the caretaker, and that was reason enough.

"All right," Lucy said, rising. "You get Fennish back to the hiding spot, and I'll get him a can of chicken soup. That's what you give people when they're sick, so I don't see why rats should be any different."

Lucy moved to the library doors, and Torsten scampered

after her. "I'll help you, Miss Lucy."

"It's still not safe to be roaming about the house, Torsten," Meridian said. "Being in the library with the doors closed is one thing. But that lantern has been on, and the burner there on the table. Tempus Crow may have seen the light."

Torsten chuckled. "You worry too much, Meridian," he said, pushing open the doors with his nose. "Miss Lucy will protect me, and maybe I can have a look at the clock to see what's wrong—"

At that moment, with an ear-splitting *"Caw!"* Tempus Crow swooped down from the shadows and snatched up Torsten in his claws. Lucy and the animals shrieked. "Got YOU—*caw!*" the crow exclaimed, and then the little dog was gone, the sound of his howls fading as the giant bird flew with him through the house.

"Torsten!" Lucy cried, and, in a panic, rushed after him. The lights in the house flickered red, the walls creaked and groaned, and the clock, Lucy registered dimly, began to tick again!

"Help me, help me, Miss Lucy!" Torsten howled.

The lights blinked on for a moment longer, and Lucy burst into the foyer just in time to see the shadowy shape of Tempus Crow disappearing into the clock.

The mechanical room door was still closed.

But the door for the cuckoo bird was open.

ELEVEN

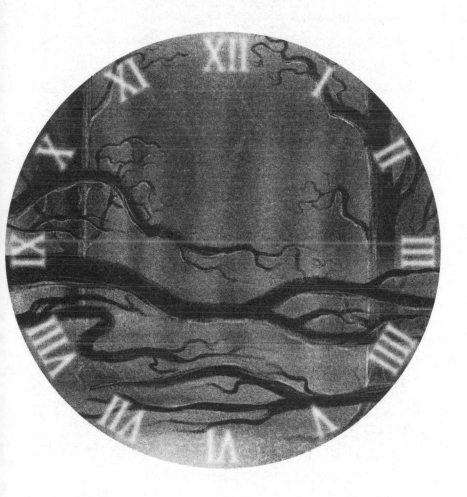

LUCY MEETS THE GARR

"Please, wake up, Fennish!" Lucy cried, setting him down on the window seat.

The burner and the lantern had been extinguished, but the library was bright with moonlight. Meridian and Nessie stood guard with their ears to the library doors, while Reginald paced nervously back and forth on the hearth. The lights were off again, and the clock had stopped ticking. Everyone was in a panic—Torsten was gone!

"Please, Fennish!" Lucy said, on the verge of tears. "Tempus Crow snatched Torsten! We need to find him!"

The rat's one eye fluttered open, catching the moonlight. "Water," he rasped. Lucy knelt and gave him a sip from the coffeepot. "Where am I?"

Meridian rushed over. "You're home, old friend," she said, leaping up onto the window seat. "Miss Lucy here is the new caretaker. She cured you with sunstone cream. But Torsten—"

"Do you know where Tempus Crow has taken him?" Lucy asked.

"The Garr," growled Fennish, trying to rise, and Meridian gently laid her paw on his shoulder.

"You're still too weak," she said, but the rat shook her off and, sitting up, turned his one eye toward the window.

"He wants our fear," Fennish said, his voice hoarse.

"Fear sows the seed—the Shadow Woods feed on fear—"

Fennish coughed, and Lucy gave him some more water.

"What do you mean, Fennish?" Meridian asked.

"That's why the Garr is snatching us. The others—they are still in the woods. Fear gives him strength. Their fear makes the Shadow Woods grow!"

"He's gone delirious again—*oink!*" Reginald said, and Meridian held up her paw to silence him.

"Are you saying the others are still alive?" the cat asked, and Fennish nodded. The animals gasped.

"The Garr is holding them prisoner," Fennish said. "He is keeping them alive, stoking their fear until the Shadow Woods consume the house."

"We were wrong, then," Nessie said. "The Garr doesn't want us dead—he wants us alive and in the Shadow Woods!"

"But how did you escape?" Meridian asked.

"I squeezed through the bars of my cage," the rat said, his one eye narrowing. "And then the Garr chased me."

The animals regarded one another nervously.

"I made it to the river. Just before dawn. And then Tempus Crow snatched me up again. But I bit him in his weak spot—where I wounded him the night he snatched me from the house—and he dropped me in the river. Not even the Garr could touch me there."

"That is why the Garr cannot leave the woods," Nessie

said to Lucy. "The same reason he cannot enter the house. The rivers and the lake are filled with sunstones—they surround the Shadow Woods on all sides."

"I turned wooden again soon after and spent that first day underwater. Tempus Crow couldn't find me and eventually gave me up for dead."

"But how did you get back inside the house?" Meridian asked.

"I followed the river to the old stone bridge. There is a hidden tunnel underneath. The house showed it to me one night when I was stealing the clocksmith's food. I made it back inside, but then . . . Forgive me, I feel faint. . . ."

"Give him something to eat," Meridian said, and with trembling hands, Lucy held the bowl of Spam to the rat's mouth. Fennish nibbled slowly at first and then faster— probably *too* fast, Lucy thought, but she needed to find out where Tempus Crow had taken Torsten. She had to rescue him and the others! But how? Lucy was on her own. Even if she told Oliver and her father—and even if they believed her—they would never agree to a trip into the Shadow Woods to fight a ten-foot-tall tree man.

"That's enough, old friend," Meridian said, gently nudging the bowl away, and the rat sat back on his hindquarters and licked his chops.

"I feel much better now, thank you."

"Fennish," Lucy said, forcing herself to keep calm, "do you know where the Garr is keeping Torsten and the other animals?"

"A giant shelter made of branches deep within the woods. The cages are inside. But Tempus Crow—if he saw me in here, if he tells the Garr I'm alive, he might have to kill the others. Indeed, I fear he may have killed them already. My escape surely has given them hope, and hope is the antidote to fear."

Reginald and Nessie moaned in despair.

"Torsten's done for—*oink!* We need to get back to the hiding spot before Tempus Crow comes back—*oink-oink!*"

"I'm afraid he's right," Nessie said, hopping closer. "There's nothing we can do for the others. And now that Tempus Crow knows we're in the library, it's only a matter of time before he finds the hiding spot!"

"You don't understand," said Fennish, slipping onto the floor. "The Garr *wants* us to hide. The more we fear, the closer the Shadow Woods creep toward the house. The clock is broken—nothing can protect us!"

"Miss Lucy's family is here to fix the clock," Meridian said. "Lucy is the caretaker. She got it ticking again, with love. But our fear must have stopped it. But it *is* working, Fennish—only the lights are red."

Fennish's one eye narrowed. "*Red*, you say?"

157

"This is no time to worry about the clock!" Lucy cried. "We've got to save Torsten and the others!"

"What?" Nessie cried. "Fennish said the others are probably dead. And Torsten—it's only a matter of time before the Garr kills him, too."

"The Garr wants his fear," Fennish said. "He will keep him alive long enough to nourish the Shadow Woods. As for the others, we can't give up on them. There is still hope they are alive."

"Which means I have to try to save them," Lucy said, moving to the door.

"But, Miss Lucy, that's suicide," said Nessie. "At least wait until daybreak. The Garr isn't around during the day."

"We don't have time to wait. Their lives are in danger."

Reginald gasped. "You're out of your mind. The Garr will just kill you, too—*oink-oink!*"

"The Garr can't cross the river," Lucy said. "But we need to go now. Time is wasting. Fennish—that hidden tunnel that leads to the bridge—can a human fit inside?"

The rat nodded.

"But even if you escape the Garr," said Nessie, "you'll still have Tempus Crow to contend with."

"The lantern," Lucy said. "Maybe if we turn it on again it will draw his attention back to the house."

"You'd risk your life to save us?" asked Fennish Seven.

"Well, I *am* the caretaker, aren't I?"

"That you are," said the rat. "However, you will never find the Garr's lair on your own. I must go with you."

"No, you're still too weak," Meridian said. "Just tell me the way and I shall go."

"There's no time to waste getting lost," said Fennish, moving to the door. "Miss Lucy can carry me if I get too tired."

There was a bit more back and forth about what to do and how to do it, but soon the matter was settled, and Lucy and Fennish slipped from the library precisely at one o'clock by Oliver's watch. Miraculously, he'd slept through the chaos, but still, Lucy thought it best not to waste time or risk waking him by changing out of her nightgown.

Armed with only a fire poker for protection and with Oliver's watch to light her way, Lucy grabbed her flip-flops from the foyer and joined Fennish at the massive fireplace in the parlor. The rat pressed three dark stones in the hearth floor with his nose, and with a deep scraping sound, the left inside wall of the fireplace swung open inwardly.

"Watch your head," Fennish said, disappearing inside. Lucy turned on the flashlight in Oliver's watch and thrust her wrist into the cavity, where she spied some stone steps curving down into the darkness. The space was much too cramped for her to stand, so Lucy swung herself in feetfirst, slipped down a few steps on her backside, then pushed the secret door closed behind her and descended to the bottom of the narrow shaft. Fennish was waiting for her at the mouth of the tunnel.

"It is about three hundred yards to the river," Fennish said, his one eye twinkling in the light from Oliver's watch.

Her heart pounding, Lucy followed Fennish into the tunnel with the poker at her side and Oliver's watch held out in front of her. The air was thick and musty, and the clopping of her flip-flops was so loud that after a few steps Lucy took them off. The stone floor was cold and damp, and the watch cast creepy, sweeping shadows on the walls. Lucy's legs felt as if they weighed a hundred pounds each, but somehow she kept them moving, her eyes never leaving Fennish, whose long, thin tail she could just make out at the edge of her light ahead.

After about a minute, the rat asked if he could rest, upon which Lucy scooped him up and carried him along with her flip-flips and the poker. His breathing had grown shallow, and she could feel the rat's heart pounding against her side. The journey to the river was only the length of three football fields, Lucy kept telling herself, but it seemed to take forever, until finally, the tunnel began to narrow sharply.

"Douse your light," Fennish said, leaping from her arms. Lucy flicked off Oliver's watch, and soon she was crawling on her hands and knees, dragging the poker and her flip-flops along the stone floor as quietly as she could. The tunnel narrowed to about three feet in diameter, and then Lucy spied some dim strands of moonlight filtering through an iron grate up ahead.

"The bridge," Fennish whispered. He pushed open the grate, which was hinged like the window in the mechanical room, and he disappeared into the night. Lucy squeezed through the opening after him and, sliding down the muddy riverbank on her stomach, splashed into the water under the bridge. Lucy sat up. The water was unexpectedly warm and shallow, rising only to her thighs, but still Lucy shivered in the cool night air, her skin popping at once into gooseflesh under her dampened nightgown.

"The path to the Garr's lair is only half a mile that way," Fennish whispered, jerking his muzzle upstream. "And yet I fear I haven't the strength to make the journey after all."

"Then I will carry you," Lucy said. She slipped on her flip-flops and scooped up the rat again into her arms.

Gripping the poker tightly, Lucy ducked out from under the bridge. The babbling, moonlit stream looked like molten silver flowing around the black sunstones.

"Of course," Lucy muttered, glancing up at the darkened underside of the bridge. It, too, she now realized, was made of sunstones.

Lucy tromped through the water to the bank opposite the Shadow Woods and began moving against the gentle current, keeping to the shadows as best she could. After a short distance, the insides of her toes began to hurt and Lucy took off her flip-flops. Fennish held them in his teeth as Lucy hopped from stone to stone, using the poker as a walking stick. Often, she would stop and listen, her eyes, her ears ever vigilant for any sign of Tempus Crow or the Garr. She could hear all sorts of night noises in the woods to her right; but to her left, on the far side of the narrow river, the Shadow Woods loomed lifeless and silent in a seamless wall of black.

They traveled in silence for about fifteen minutes, and then Fennish told Lucy to stop. Lucy slipped on her flip-flops again and looked around. In the Shadow Woods to her left, she could see a murky opening in the trees like the tunnel of branches behind the house. Lucy had broken a sweat hurrying along the riverbank, but all at once it seemed her body heat—and her courage—began to evaporate.

Lucy shivered. She could hardly believe she was here. Three days ago, her biggest fear had been missing out on a summer back home with her friends. And now here she was, the caretaker of a magical house on a mission with a magical rat to save a bunch of magical animals from a magical tree monster who lived in some magical woods.

A sob rose in Lucy's throat; and suddenly, more than anything, she missed her mother. The missing always came on her like that—powerfully and when she least expected it—but tonight, Lucy wondered if her mother could see her. Was she mad at her for what she was doing? Was she proud? And then there was Oliver and Pop. Had they awakened to find her missing? And what would become of them if she didn't come back? Was this whole trip a fool's errand?

"Are you all right, Miss Lucy?" Fennish asked, and Lucy squeezed her eyes shut. She *would* come back—so would the animals—and when Lucy looked again at the Shadow Woods, a strange calm came over her. Just like her mother had been her caretaker until she got sick, Lucy was now the caretaker for the animals. And that meant she was right where she needed to be.

"I'm fine," Lucy said, gripping the poker tightly, and she glanced at Oliver's watch—1:32. Meridian had suggested they wait at least twenty minutes before turning on the lantern. "Do you think it's been long enough now?"

"We can only hope," Fennish said. "But be ready to run at any moment."

Lucy nodded, and with a deep breath, she tromped across the river and carried Fennish up the bank into the Shadow Woods.

The darkness consumed them at once, and after a few

yards, Lucy could no longer hear the river at all—only the soft crunch of her footsteps along the forest bed. The calm she had felt only seconds before was replaced with a heart-hammering dread. The hairs on her neck bristled. Behind her was a jagged patch of moonlight, and up ahead a curtain of unbroken gloom. Lucy turned on Oliver's watch-light.

"You'll give us away!" Fennish hissed, and Lucy quickened her pace.

"I need to see where I'm going!" she hissed back, aiming the light on the path, but still, much of it spilled over into the woods around her. The trees looked almost alive in the passing shadows, their branches poised like tentacles ready to snatch them at any moment into the darkness.

Lucy moaned in fright and broke into a run, holding the poker out in front of her like a hunter, and after fifty yards or so, Fennish cried, "There!"

The rat leaped from her arms, and Lucy shone her light after him.

"I'll release the others from their cages," Fennish said—he was now standing in the opening of a tall wigwam-like dwelling that disappeared up into the trees. "You keep watch out here. Any sign of Tempus Crow or the Garr, you make a run for the river, you understand?"

Lucy nodded, and as Fennish slipped inside the wigwam, Lucy trained her light up along the side of it. Branches arched down from the forest canopy in such a way that it was hard to tell where the wigwam began and the trees ended—and not only that, the structure appeared to be at the intersection of three tunnels. One was the tunnel down which they had just traveled; another, Lucy figured, must lead back toward the house; and the last— Well, Lucy had no desire to find out where *that* tunnel led.

"Go, go, get to the river!" Fennish cried, emerging from the wigwam. The missing animals poured out a second later and hurried past Lucy down the path. Lucy recognized all of them from their holes in the clock as they passed: the beaver, the squirrel, the raccoon, the skunk, the fawn, the duck, and finally the turtle, which Lucy remembered went in the *five* hole.

But where was Torsten Six?

Lucy froze, and as if on cue, the little dog cried for help from somewhere deep within the woods. A heavy rumbling and the crack of snapping branches followed, and then a thunderous voice bellowed: *"I WANT YOUR FEAR, TORSTEN SIX!"*

The earth shook with a quickening *boom, boom, boom!* The Garr's footsteps, Lucy understood with dawning horror. And they were getting closer!

"Oh no," Fennish cried, coming back. "He's chasing him like he chased me!"

"The Garr's been frightening us senseless ever since you escaped," said the turtle, who had made it only a few steps down the path.

"*HELP! HELP!*" the little dog screamed, and the Garr howled with laughter.

"We've got to save him!" Lucy cried, and Fennish snarled.

"You get Frederick Five here and the others across the river," the rat said, nudging Lucy toward the turtle. "I'll distract the Garr."

"But Fennish," Lucy protested, "you're still weak!"

"Aye, but now I'm angry, too," the rat growled. "Now *go!*"

Lucy picked up the turtle and raced down the path after the other animals. She caught up with them at the edge of the woods, and together everyone slid down the embankment and splashed across the river as the Garr bellowed and boomed behind them.

"Oh, thank you, thank you!" the animals cried, and then Torsten screamed: "*HELP ME, PLEASE!*"

He was closer now, Lucy realized as the *boom, boom, boom*s grew louder. A moment later, the little dog's dim shape appeared at the edge of the woods.

"Hurry, Torsten, run!" Lucy cried, splashing back out into the river, and before she realized what was happening, Tempus Crow appeared from nowhere and dove straight for her.

"Look out!" one of the animals cried, and everything next happened in a blur. Lucy dropped the turtle and swung the poker, knocking Tempus Crow out of sight into the shadows. At the same time, Torsten leaped from the riverbank and knocked Lucy backward into the water. The fire poker went flying, and Torsten splashed up into Lucy's lap. He was shaking, and his eyes were wide with terror.

"It's the Garr, the Garr! He's coming after us!" Torsten cried. More booming and snapping of branches, and then Fennish leaped out of the woods and tumbled down the riverbank. At the same time, a monstrous, hand-shaped branch exploded out of the woods, nearly snatching him; and Fennish splashed head over tail into the water. Lucy scrambled after him, scooped up the rat into her arms along with Torsten, and quickly joined the other animals on the opposite riverbank.

"The Garr," Frederick Five whispered, his head retracting back into his shell, and Lucy found a pair of glowing red eyes the size of footballs glaring back at her from across the river. The clock animals shuddered and moaned, and then the Garr's giant, egg-shaped head and massive shoulders emerged from the woods. Even in the moonlight, Lucy could see the monster's skin was made of bark.

The Garr tentatively reached for the river, his fingers

barely touching the water, and then *hisssssssssss!* The Garr shrieked, snatching back his hand as if he'd touched a hot stove. He zeroed his red eyes on Lucy and growled—low and creaking like tree limbs in the wind.

"GIVE ME BACK MY ANIMALS," the Garr croaked, and his lips parted to reveal dozens of jagged black teeth against a wide, fiery crescent of a mouth.

Lucy, her throat tight with terror, clutched Fennish and Torsten tightly to her chest and shook her head.

The Garr gave a deafening roar and then, without warning, grabbed a nearby tree trunk and snapped it in half.

"RUN!" Fennish cried, leaping from Lucy's arms. Torsten dove after him, Lucy grabbed Frederick, and everyone scrambled up the riverbank into the woods. A moment later, the ground shook with the thundering slam of the shadow wood tree behind them. Bright-orange light flooded everything, and Lucy felt a blast of heat on her back.

Lucy whirled—the shadow wood tree had burst into flames—but then, just as quickly, the flames burned out, the tree crumbled, and its ashes were swept away into the river. The Garr howled in frustration.

"The sunstone," Fennish said, breathless, and he collapsed at Lucy's feet. Lucy set down Frederick, picked up Fennish, and with sudden rage, shouted across the river: "You stay away from our house!"

The Garr roared at Lucy hatefully, then shrank back into the Shadow Woods. Branches snapped, the monster's red eyes blinked out, and in the next moment, there was only the babbling of the river and the pounding of Lucy's heart.

"Fennish," said Torsten, panting with fright, "he distracted the Garr so I could make it to the river—but I fear the monster wounded him again."

"Poor old Fennish," said Frederick, peeking out from his shell. "Is he—?"

The turtle couldn't bring himself to say *"dead,"* and the other animals gazed up at Lucy anxiously, their eyes little more than smudges in the shadows at the edge of the woods. Lucy pressed her ear against Fennish's side. His breathing was shallow, but his heartbeat was steady.

"He'll be okay," Lucy said, stroking the rat's head. "We're going home now. All of us. We're going home."

TWELVE

TEDDY'S REVENGE

Oliver awoke that morning to the blinding glare of sunlight in his eyes. It had to be after eight o'clock, but he couldn't tell for sure because his watch was missing and Lucy was still asleep in her bed. Oliver slipped on his glasses—wait, Lucy *was not* asleep in her bed. It was just the lump of her pillow between the sheets.

Oliver quickly got dressed and, slipping across the hallway into the bathroom, checked his face in the mirror. It was as he feared. There were two new pimples on his forehead, and his chin looked worse. Oliver sighed.

"Idiot," he muttered. Next time Teddy gave him an acorn, he would use the same amount of dust that he'd used when he rubbed it on his face by accident. No more, no less. And no sunstone cream either, no matter how badly it itched. That had to be the reason why the pimples were coming back. The jar's label said sunstone cream counteracted the effects of shadow wood.

Oliver washed his face and padded out into the kitchen, where he found his father fixing a cup of coffee.

"Looks like we all slept in," he said, and Oliver asked where Lucy was. "She's still curled up in the library, dead to the world."

"The *library*?" Oliver asked, pushing up his glasses.

"I found her in there this morning when I went looking

for my coffeepot and burner." Mr. Tinker tapped the metal rack with his spoon. "How much you want to bet your snoring kept her awake last night? Or maybe it was mine. I *have* been known to saw some wood in my time."

Mr. Tinker chuckled, but Oliver frowned. He'd been the last one to use the burner in the kitchen when he'd heated up some water to wash his face the night before. That meant Lucy must have taken the burner and the coffeepot into the library when she went in there to sleep. But why?

"Well, let her sleep a little longer," said Mr. Tinker, pouring his coffee into his travel mug. "I was going to drag you guys on some more errands, but let me head out now, okay? Lucy was miserable yesterday and—well, would you mind holding down the fort here while I'm gone? I won't be long, and I'll pick up a pizza for lunch."

As Mr. Tinker consulted a list he'd set on the counter, Oliver quietly made his way to the library and cracked open the doors. One of the big leather chairs had been moved so it faced the hearth, and there was Lucy, fast asleep under a blanket with that stupid dog statue again under her arm. Oliver sniffed at the air. The library smelled of that stinky sunstone cream and something else—was it tuna fish?—and there were empty bowls on the floor in front of the fireplace. What the heck had Lucy been up to last night?

"*Psst!*" Oliver turned to find his father glaring angrily

at him from the foyer. He jerked his thumb for Oliver to get out of there, and Oliver gently closed the doors. A minute later, he was on the front porch, waving goodbye as his father's truck sputtered out of sight into the Shadow Woods at the end of the driveway.

The Shadow Woods.

Oliver thought they looked closer but couldn't tell for sure—not the way he could when he looked at the carriage house—and so he bounded off the porch and around back to check. Oliver sighed. The carriage house looked much the same—maybe a few more saplings here and there—but nothing major, he thought.

"Why didn't you use the acorn?"

Oliver whirled. It was Teddy, calling to him from the edge of the Shadow Woods. But as Oliver drew closer, he noticed that Teddy's fists were clenched, and his eyes were hard with anger.

"When someone gives you a gift, it's an insult not to use it," Teddy said, and Oliver stopped a couple of yards away from him. There was an edge in Teddy's voice that made him nervous. "Your face is a mess. Why didn't you use the acorn?"

"I *did* use it," Oliver said, his voice cracking. "I used too much, in fact, and had to apply some cream to stop the itching."

Teddy narrowed his eyes suspiciously. "What kind of cream?"

An image of the acorn sizzling on the path flashed through Oliver's mind, and for some reason, he thought it best not to tell Teddy about the sunstone cream.

"Calamine lotion," Oliver said instead. Teddy scowled and dropped his eyes as if he was trying to think fast on his feet.

"Where's your sister?" he asked finally.

"She's still sleeping."

"Oh, I'll wager she is," Teddy said, smiling bitterly. "Busy, busy, busy. Did she tell you what she did last night?"

"What do you mean?" Oliver asked, his stomach twisting with dread, and Teddy's demeanor changed instantly. He looked almost guilty.

"Well, I don't want to get her into trouble . . ."

"Get her into trouble for *what*?" Oliver asked, his voice cracking.

"It's better if I show you."

Teddy stepped aside and gestured for Oliver to enter past him into the woods. Oliver pushed up his glasses. His heart was pounding now, and the back of his neck prickled with the premonition that something very bad was about to happen.

"I—er—I can't," Oliver stammered. "I have to keep an eye

on Lucy while our father is at the store. What did she do?"

"She stole something very important to me," Teddy said, his eyes again growing angry, and Oliver's head was suddenly swimming.

"What are you talking about? Lucy's never stolen anything in her life."

"The Shadow Woods have a strange effect on people. You should know that better than anyone, Oliver Tinker." Teddy gestured again for Oliver to enter the woods. "Come, let me show you what she did."

Oliver's feet remained rooted to the spot. "Just tell me what she stole."

"She broke into my house and stole my statues," Teddy said deliberately, as if spelling it out for a child. "But she didn't steal *all* of them. There is still one statue left. The cuckoo bird."

"Wait—you mean the clock animals?" Teddy nodded. "But why do *you* have—"

"Because they're a nuisance!" Teddy spat. "Just like your sister. She thinks she's so smart, but without the cuckoo bird, you Tinkers will never get that clock ticking again—not the way you want. Now how about you march that pimply face of yours back into the house and bring me what's rightfully mine?"

Oliver was so shocked he couldn't speak and just shook

his head, *"No."* Teddy smiled.

"I see, then," he said quietly. "You've known all along that the animals power the clock, haven't you? But they power much more than that, and now that they're back in the house, I'm afraid I need to change my plans before your father learns the truth."

Teddy produced an acorn from his pocket and held it between his thumb and forefinger as if he were saying *"Okay?"*—but Oliver suddenly knew that things were *not* okay. Every fiber in his body screamed at him to run, but before Oliver could move his legs, the world dimmed, and something crunched and crackled behind him.

Oliver spun around, and his heart seized in terror. Whereas only moments before he had been standing at the edge of the Shadow Woods, Oliver was now standing *inside* them, a whole ten yards or so down the path. And there, silhouetted against the mouth of the tunnel of branches, was Teddy, blocking his way back toward the house.

Oliver's eyes bulged in disbelief.

"You Tinkers are tinkering with things you do not understand," Teddy said, stepping closer, and a large crow swooped down from the trees and lighted on his shoulder. Oliver could not see the bird clearly in the shadows, but for some reason, he felt sure it was the same crow that had pooped all over Theo and Betty Bigsby.

But that's impossible, Oliver told himself, backing away—*all of this* was impossible—and then the crow spread its wings and lurched toward him.

"Boo!"

Oliver shrieked and took off down the path, fully aware that he was running *into* the Shadow Woods. And yet Oliver kept running; his only thought was that he needed to get away. An image of his mother in the graveyard flashed before his eyes—yes, the crow had been there in his nightmare, too, he now remembered. But this was no nightmare; this was *real.*

Oliver was so terrified that he could hardly breathe, and what little air entered his nostrils smelled of rotting leaves and garbage. The trees dissolved into a wall of murk rushing past, and soon, he could barely see ten feet ahead.

Oliver slowed down and glanced behind him. Teddy and the crow were gone, but before Oliver had time to process what had happened, he came to a wide, cylindrical structure made of branches. Oliver dimly registered that it resembled a nuclear reactor—except at the top, where the branches blended in with the forest canopy.

Oliver leaned against a tree to catch his breath. The smell of garbage here was nauseating, but now that his eyes had adjusted to the dark, he could see the structure was at the intersection of three tunnels—one of which was behind him. The second tunnel was little more than a gaping black hole among the trees, but at the end of the third, Oliver spied a swatch of daylight. And was that the river he heard, too?

Oliver instinctively made a break for it—when from out of the shadows, Teddy appeared on the path in front of him. Oliver shrieked—*This can't be happening*, his mind told him—but before he could run, Teddy waved his hand, and a pair of branches reached down and seized Oliver by the arms. He struggled and screamed for help, but the branches were as strong as iron bars.

"Tempus Crow tells me everything is almost ready," Teddy said, coming closer as the big black bird landed on his shoulder. "Another of your nightmares should've gotten the clock ticking again. After all, there is no fear as powerful, no fear as pure as a child's nightmare."

Oliver, heart pounding and head spinning, could only stand there in frozen terror as Teddy came closer. What was happening? What was Teddy talking about? This had to be a nightmare—a nightmare from which, at any moment now, he would wake up in his room at Blackford House.

Wake up, Oliver, wake up!

"But the acorns didn't work," Teddy went on. "How odd. Just a little dust on the skin is usually more than enough to provoke the worst of nightmares. Perhaps the love in the house is stronger than I thought—the sunstone, more powerful. Your sister has certainly proven herself powerful, what with her love for those clock animals. Those pesky, *rotten* clock animals."

Teddy's eyes flashed red. Oliver's only thought again was to run. But Oliver couldn't run—the Shadow Woods had him trapped.

"HELP! HELP!" Oliver cried.

"No one can hear you scream in the Shadow Woods," Teddy said, only inches away now. "But your family will hear you scream tonight—in the house, when the acorn gives you your final and most terrifying nightmare. The clock will start ticking again, and the Shadow Woods will carry me home. After all, fear is always stronger in the end."

Teddy smiled, and despite his terror, Oliver somehow understood. The clock was a perpetual motion clock. The shadow wood in the house reacted to the atmospheric changes caused by fear. The sunstone in the clock face was the counterbalance—a counterbalance to the animal statues, which were made from shadow wood. The sunstone cream worked the same way: it balanced out the acorn dust. *That* was why he didn't have any nightmares last night—which meant Oliver had been right all along. The pipes were *supposed* to connect to the animals in the clock face. The clock face was made of sunstone, and the animals were shadow wood batteries!

All this flashed through Oliver's terrified mind in a millisecond, along with the dawning realization that the whole story about Teddy's father nearly blowing up the house had been a lie. Teddy had no father, and there was no caretaker's cottage out here either—only this strange dwelling in which there lived a horrible boy and his crow.

"Who are you?" Oliver asked weakly.

Teddy held the acorn closer, and it burst apart into a teeming tangle of twisting black roots. Oliver made to scream, but then the acorn leaped from Teddy's hand and clamped over Oliver's mouth like an octopus seizing its prey. There was a brief, mind-shattering moment of unimaginable horror in which Oliver's muffled cries were choked off by the acorn slithering down his throat. And then, mercifully, the darkness dragged him under, and Oliver Tinker knew nothing more.

THIRTEEN

THE NIGHTMARE BEGINS

*K*nock-knock-knock!

Lucy's eyes snapped open.

"Rise and shine, slacker," her father called from the parlor. "It's lunchtime."

Lucy sat up and blinked around the library. Sleep had come to her in what felt like a long, dreamless jump, and now it was almost noon. She was still wearing Oliver's watch, and Torsten was still tucked beside her in the chair.

Lucy shivered and swiveled her eyes out the window. There was a monster living less than thirty yards away from her in the Shadow Woods. A ten-foot-tall tree man with eyes like fire and a glowing mouth full of fangs. The Garr. He was more terrifying than Lucy could have ever imagined—and boy had she made him angry.

Lucy pulled Torsten close. The Garr would have killed them all if not for the sunstone in the river. There was comfort in knowing that there was sunstone in the house, too—that should keep the Garr away—but was it right to keep all this secret, especially from Oliver, who had become friends with a kid who lived in the Shadow Woods? Was Lucy endangering everyone by not telling them the truth about this place?

Lucy sighed and rubbed her eyes. She hadn't had a good night's sleep since they arrived, and it was getting hard to think straight. At least the animals were all safe now, she told herself, eyeing the bookcase near the fireplace. Lucy had been right all along. The hiding spot was behind the bookcase.

Lucy swung her legs out of the chair and winced. Her lower back ached, her knees were sore from crawling in the tunnel, and her toes stung from tromping through the brush along the riverbank in her flip-flops. Lucy and the animals had made it to the stone bridge and safely back into the house long before sunrise—and with no sign of Tempus Crow, thank you very much. Lucy had whacked him silly with the fire poker, after all—but was he dead or just injured?

And then there was Fennish, the real hero, who had nearly died from exhaustion. And after reuniting the animals in the library, Lucy nursed him back to health again with a dab of sunstone cream and more food and water. Lucy fed the rest of the animals, too; and when it was clear that Fennish would pull through—at about four o'clock, by Oliver's watch—everyone returned to the hiding spot. Except for Torsten. He was still so terrified, he refused to leave Lucy's side. Meridian allowed him to remain there only if Lucy swore never to let him leave her sight. And with that, Lucy and the little dog had fallen asleep in the chair.

"Don't worry," she whispered in Torsten's wooden ear.

"Everything is going to be all right."

Lucy looked down at her nightgown and frowned. It was all sooty and gray from the secret passage in the fireplace. In fact, sitting there in the sunlight, *everything* from the night before seemed sooty and gray, close and yet far away—like the Shadow Woods outside the window. And on top of it all, Lucy was starving.

Lucy tucked Torsten under her arm and hurried through the house into the kitchen, where she found her father washing his hands at the sink. His back was to her, so he didn't notice what a mess she was.

"I guess Ollie's snoring kept you awake last night, huh?" he said, chuckling. Oliver didn't even acknowledge her. He was sitting at the table, his eyes fixed on the pizza box in front of him.

Lucy muttered a reply, darted into her bedroom for some clothes, and then dashed across the hallway into the bathroom, where she threw a towel over Torsten for privacy and showered. The cold water made her feel better for once. Lucy quickly dressed and braided her hair, then tucked Torsten under her arm and hurried back out into the kitchen.

The others had already started on the pizza—pepperoni and mushrooms, Lucy's favorite—so she set the statue of Torsten on the counter and joined them at the table. Her father barely noticed—he was more concerned with Oliver.

"You sure you don't want any pizza, Ollie?" he said, and Oliver shook his head. He looked tired, and his color was pale. Mr. Tinker felt his forehead. "You don't have a fever or anything."

"What's going on?" Lucy asked, digging into her pizza.

"Ollie's got a stomachache. Poor kid said he felt dizzy after I left and spent the whole morning sitting on the porch. I found him there when I got home. Must've eaten something that disagreed with him—unless you've been messing with those acorns again. Don't tell me you ate one or something, Ollie."

Mr. Tinker chuckled, but Oliver didn't think it was funny. He furrowed his brow as if trying to remember something, then pushed up his glasses and shook his head.

"I'll be fine. I'm just not hungry."

"Well, you take it easy today," said Mr. Tinker, munching away. "The pendulum is oiled and ready to go. I've just got to figure out a way to modify it so the winding mechanism doesn't throw off the electromagnetic current."

"What do you mean?" Lucy asked, and her father raised his eyebrow.

"Since when are you interested in clocks?"

Lucy shrugged. "Just bored I guess," she lied—Lucy really wanted to know what was going on so Torsten could hear, too. "I thought the pendulum was the problem. Isn't it rusted or something?"

Mr. Tinker chuckled. "Well, sort of. Ollie and I think the electromagnetic balance is off within the clock, which means the pendulum is . . . well, *frozen*. Think of it as a giant magnet holding it in place. So, Ollie and I are going to build a custom winding mechanism that . . . well, you remember that time the truck's battery died and that guy gave me a jump start?" Lucy nodded. "The winding mechanism will work like that. It will jump-start the clock, which will generate enough electromagnetic current from the shadow wood to keep the clock ticking. Does that make sense?"

"I think so," Lucy said. "Why can't you just, you know, start the pendulum yourself or something? That would start the magic—I mean, er—the magnetic current from the shadow wood, right?"

"The magnetic force holding it in place is too strong. You'd need six football players up there to get it swinging. Not to mention, what do you do if the clock stops again? You need a winding mechanism with enough torque to get things started, then to act as a fail-safe in case the clock stops." Mr. Tinker chewed on his pizza. "Matter of fact, if the clock had been built with a winding mechanism in the first place, Mr. Quigley wouldn't be in this mess. He could just turn a crank and, bingo, the clock would start again.

There's no such thing as a true perpetual motion clock."

There was that term again—perpetual motion—but Lucy got the gist of what her father was saying. And hopefully Torsten had gotten the gist of it, too. The pendulum wasn't rusted or broken or anything; it was just frozen and needed a jump start to get the magic flowing through the pipes—a jump start from either her caretaking or the winding mechanism. Let her father call it electromagnetic current or whatever. Lucy knew the truth, and that was all that mattered. She winked at Torsten.

"You know, I really wish you'd stop messing around with Mr. Quigley's stuff," said her father, following her gaze. "What happens if you break that stupid dog statue?"

Lucy felt caught, and her cheeks grew hot. "Er—I just like him is all. He makes sleeping here not so scary."

"Oh yeah? And is that what you were trying to do to Ollie and me? Scare us this morning when we went up into the clock?"

"What are you talking about?"

"That goofy rat with the eye patch," said Lucy's father, and her stomach dropped. "Very funny hanging him from the pipes like that. But I'm telling you, stop messing around with Mr. Quigley's statues. And you stay out of the clock, too. Ollie and I have got enough on our hands without you breaking something."

Lucy glanced across the table at Oliver, who just sat there as if in a daze, and then back at Torsten. It was clear to her what had happened. For some reason, Fennish had gone up into the clock after returning to the hiding spot. But how? And why would he risk his life all over again by turning wooden *in the clock*—just a few feet away from the window through which Tempus Crow had been entering the house? After all, no one knew for sure what had happened to him!

Lucy's heart was pounding with panic, but she forced a chuckle that sounded fake even to her. "Okay, okay, if you can't take a joke. You're right, I shouldn't have been messing around in the clock. Where is the rat statue now? I'll put him back where he belongs. Same with Torsten."

"What?" her father asked, and Lucy, caught again, felt her cheeks go even hotter.

"Er—that's what I named the dog. Torsten."

Lucy's father chuckled. "For a minute I thought you said *torsion*. Which is pretty funny. A torsion pendulum is what's normally used in a perpetual motion clock, right, Ollie?"

Oliver smiled vaguely, as if he were only half paying attention, and turned his eyes toward the window. Lucy could tell something was bothering him, but she had bigger fish to fry: Fennish had gone up into the clock last night after their adventure in the Shadow Woods, and Lucy needed to figure out why.

"Er—where'd you put the rat, Pop?" she asked, scooping up Torsten. Her father jerked his chin at the dining room, and Lucy hurried inside. She found Fennish on the table. His body was contorted as if he had turned wooden in the middle of a jumping jack, and his face was twisted and tense with strain.

"What the heck were you doing in the clock?" Lucy whispered, but the statue's expression remained the same. Lucy sighed and picked him up. "All right, I'll wait until midnight to find out. Meantime, let's get you both back into the library."

As Lucy turned to leave with Fennish and Torsten, she noticed something strange in the painting of Blackford House over the buffet: the faint, almost ghostlike outlines of three figures standing on the front steps. There was also the outline of a figure in the horse-drawn carriage driver's seat. Perhaps she hadn't noticed them before, but after what she'd learned about the paintings of Edgar Blackford . . .

The back of Lucy's neck prickled, and she hurried into the library, where she placed Torsten and Fennish on the hearth and plopped down again in the big leather armchair.

And that is where Lucy sat for most of day, reading books and staring out at the Shadow Woods. The only time she left the library was just before supper, when she saw Oliver walk past the big windows for the tenth time. He'd been circling the house for more than twenty minutes wearing a pained expression, as if he were lost.

Lucy tucked Torsten and Fennish under her arms and slipped out onto the porch, where she waited for Oliver to come around again. And when he did, Lucy stopped him and asked what he was doing.

"I'm retracing my steps," he said, looking around, and Lucy blinked at him, confused. She thought his color looked better, but he seemed antsy, and his voice sounded weak. "This morning, before my stomach started bothering me, I remember waving to Pop from the porch as he drove off, and then I went around back to check the carriage house and—"

Oliver broke off in thought. Many years later, looking back, Lucy would wonder if things might have turned out differently if only she'd asked Oliver *why* he had checked the carriage house. At the time, Lucy had been spending so much time inside tending to the animals, she had no idea how far the Shadow Woods had advanced in only a few days. However, in that moment, eager as she was to get back to the library, Lucy assumed Oliver had gone into the carriage house for the gas cans. And so, she just stood there, waiting for him to go on.

"I think I must've gotten dizzy in the carriage house or something," he said finally. "Next thing I remember, I was on the porch again. But it couldn't have been for as long as Pop said"—Oliver wrinkled his brow, trying to remember—"or at least, it doesn't *seem* that long, looking back."

"Are you sure you're all right, Ollie?" Lucy asked.

Oliver nodded, pushed up his glasses, and set off again around the house. And once she was back inside, Lucy watched him make another ten laps past the library windows before their father called them for a supper of canned franks and beans.

Lucy ate in the library, saying that she just couldn't tear herself away from this book called *Great Expectations*. She used the same excuse to bail on another game of Monopoly. Her father was so thrilled that she was reading, he didn't even argue.

Around nine o'clock, while the others were still playing in the kitchen, Lucy brought the statues with her upstairs while she made sure that the mechanical room door was shut. She also climbed the ladder and secured the cuckoo door with an old shoelace she'd found—just in case Tempus Crow was still around.

It was after ten when the children settled into their beds, and they lay there for a long time in silence—Oliver staring up at the ceiling, and Lucy, with the statues by her side, staring at Oliver. She had managed to sneak Torsten and Fennish into the room while her father was in the bathroom, and Oliver didn't even ask about them. He'd been acting very strange all night.

"You sure you're doing okay?" Lucy asked—she could see in the moonlight that his eyes were open.

"I miss Mom," he said quietly, and Lucy's heart squeezed. Oliver always knew how to comfort Lucy when the missing became too much for her, but Lucy never knew what to say when things were the other way around.

"I know, me too" was all she came up with.

A heavy silence hung over the bedroom, and then Oliver whispered, "I'm afraid to go to sleep."

Lucy's skin broke out into gooseflesh and her heart began to beat very fast. *Not tonight,* she thought on one level. She *needed* Oliver to fall asleep. It was almost ten thirty, and she had to prepare the animals' food before they came alive. Plus, she wanted to know why Fennish went up into the clock.

"Why are you afraid?" Lucy asked, and Oliver exhaled tensely.

"Never mind," he said, rolling over on his side. "Just get some sleep."

The next hour and a half were agony as Lucy watched Oliver toss and turn until, just before midnight, he finally fell asleep. There was no time to prepare the animals' food, so Lucy slipped from her bedroom with the statues and hurried with them into the library. Torsten and Fennish came alive a few seconds later, their wooden bodies transforming into flesh and fur in Lucy's arms.

"The clock!" Fennish cried, leaping violently onto the floor, and Lucy fell backward with Torsten into the armchair. At the same time, the lower half of the bookcase beside the hearth swung open, and the rest of the clock animals poured into the library, all ten of them chastising Fennish at once for leaving the hiding spot.

"You don't understand," the rat said. "The pipes in the clock are all wrong, I was trying to pull them out—the pipes have been rerouted from the clock face into a wall of shadow wood!"

"Well, what do you expect?" said Reginald. "What, with most of us missing, *something* had to power the clock—*oink-oink!*"

"Don't you see?" Fennish said. "That's why the lights were red. It wasn't Lucy's caretaking that got the clock ticking, it was our fear. Fear feeds the shadow wood in the house just as it feeds the trees outside. The clock has been recalibrated to run on *fear!*"

"What are you talking about?" Lucy asked. "Mr. Quigley said the last clocksmith tried to reroute the pipes into the clock face and nearly blew up the house!"

"Then Mr. Quigley is either stupid or he's lying,"

Meridian said. "The pipes have always connected to the clock face. And what Fennish says makes perfect sense."

"If only we'd learned sooner what that other clocksmith had been up to," said the squirrel—his name was Samson Ten.

The duck—who went into the *two* hole and whose name was just that, Duck—began waddling back and forth in front of the hearth. "But none of us has been up into the clock in ages!" she cried. "It's too dangerous—*quack-quack!*"

"That bald old fool with the bushy white mustache!" said Nessie. "No wonder the house covered him with soot and threw that candlestick at his head. Serves him right!"

Lucy's heart froze. "What did you say?"

"Fennish had been headed back to the hiding spot," Meridian said. "And the clocksmith would have gotten him, too, but then the house distracted him with a blast of soot from the fireplace. Sent the old man into an endless fit of coughing."

"I should never have gone for him," said Fennish, shaking his head. "That's when Tempus Crow snatched me. And if I didn't know better, I would've sworn the old man and the crow had been working together."

"That was the last we saw of him—*oink!* That is, after the house chased him away. Hit the old codger square in the head with a candlestick—*oink-oink!*"

Lucy's head was spinning. The brick that had hit Mr. Quigley's car—the house had thrown it at him. The injury to his head—that was from the candlestick. His constant coughing—that was from the soot! The house had tried to defend itself from him because *Mr. Quigley* was the former clocksmith!

"I need to tell my father," Lucy said, heading for the doors, and Meridian blocked her way. "Please, Meridian. Mr. Quigley told us he fired the last clocksmith, but Mr. Quigley *was* the last clocksmith!"

The animals shifted and muttered nervously to one another.

"Then this Mr. Quigley cannot be the caretaker!" cried Frederick the turtle.

"One thing at a time!" Fennish shouted. "We need to dismantle those pipes! If the clock should start ticking the way things are now, the magic in the shadow wood will overpower the sunstone. The trees will consume the house, and the Garr can get inside!"

"The Garr!" Torsten said, trembling. "He wants our fear! And if Mr. Quigley lied to the Tinkers, if he rerouted those pipes into the shadow wood knowing full well what it would do to the house—"

"Then that means he's been working for the Garr all along!" Lucy cried.

At that moment, a terrifying scream echoed through the darkness. The clock began its low, steady ticking, the lights flickered red and stayed on, and a low groan came from deep within the walls. The house sounded in pain.

"We're too late!" Torsten cried, and Lucy fled from the library.

FOURTEEN

BAD ALCHEMY

"Oliver!" Lucy cried, dashing through the house—the walls, the furniture, the antiques flying past her in streaks of red light and shadow. There was a low rumbling, like a train approaching, coming from outside, but Oliver would not stop screaming.

"*PLEASE, MOM, NOOOOO!*"

"Oliver!" Lucy shouted, racing through the kitchen, and then her father stepped out of his bedroom.

"What the heck is going on?" he said, still half-asleep. "Is that the—?"

Crash!—a window shattered. Lucy's father whirled, and then a cluster of shadow wood branches reached out from his bedroom and snatched him back inside.

"Pop!" Lucy cried, running after him, and then froze in horror at his door.

Dozens of shadow wood branches had broken in through her father's window. The red light spilling in from the hallway gave them the appearance of a giant hand, beneath which Mr. Tinker lay, pinned in his bed. There were smaller branches coiled around his wrists and ankles, too, and one over his mouth, gagging him.

Lucy's father screamed something unintelligible, and then one of the branches shoved Lucy backward into the hallway and slammed the door.

Howling in desperation, Lucy rammed the door with her shoulder, but the branch was bracing it shut from inside.

Crash!—more glass breaking—and then Oliver screamed, *"NO, MOM, PLEEEAAAASE!"*

Lucy moved to their bedroom door and burst inside. Oliver lay in his bed, writhing and moaning in the band of light from the hallway. More shadow wood branches scraped at the shattered window frame, and the floor was littered with shards of broken glass—which Lucy deftly avoided as she rushed to her brother's side.

"Oliver, wake up!" she cried, her eyes darting frantically between the branches and her brother. The hair around his forehead was matted and sweaty, and his cheeks were streaked with tears. Lucy shook him by the shoulders. "Oliver, please! The Shadow Woods have Pop—we need to get help!"

Oliver's eyes fluttered open, and a low moan escaped his lips.

"The acorn," he rasped weakly. "Teddy . . . he gave me the nightmares. . . ."

Oliver's head lolled on his pillow and his eyes closed. Lucy shook him by the shoulders and slapped his face. Oliver's eyes opened halfway.

"Oliver, listen to me. The clock is ticking. The shadow wood has overpowered the sunstone, and the trees are inside the house. They've got Pop!"

"The acorn . . . ," Oliver muttered, and then Lucy heard a cackle, low and croaking, coming from outside. Gazing out the window, she spied a pair of glowing red eyes staring back at her amid the trees. Lucy gasped.

It was the Garr!

"*RUN,*" he groaned, low and satisfied. "*RUN AND GIVE ME YOUR FEAR!*"

Lucy's heart nearly stopped—there was no river this time to protect her from the giant tree man—but the Garr *wanted* them to run. That's why the branches were holding back in the window. The Garr needed more fear—he could not enter the house yet. The sunstone was still too strong!

Where Lucy found the strength to carry Oliver as far as she did, she never knew. Lucy swung his arm over her shoulder, heaved him out of bed, and made it all the way into the foyer before collapsing with him onto the floor. The rumbling had stopped, but the ticking of the clock was loud and steady.

"The pendulum!" Lucy cried. Of course! If she could stop it from swinging, the Shadow Woods would stop advancing!

Lucy raced up into the mechanical room and threw her body against the swinging pendulum. But the force of it was too strong, and it knocked her backward onto her bottom.

Lucy tried again, and again the pendulum knocked her back. It was no use; she couldn't stop it alone.

Lucy howled in frustration and hurried back down to the foyer, where she found Oliver curled up in the fetal position, clutching his stomach.

"Teddy," he groaned groggily. "He gave me a night-mare . . . the acorn."

The acorn. There was only one thing Lucy knew that could counteract its effects.

Lucy rushed into the library, fetched the jar of sunstone cream, and was back in the foyer in a matter of seconds. She smeared the cream on every inch of Oliver's bare skin she could find—his neck and face, his arms, even his stomach and the soles of his feet. And after a moment, Oliver began to convulse. His eyes snapped open, and he rolled over onto his hands and knees, choking and coughing.

Lucy was certain for a moment that she'd killed him, when suddenly, Oliver coughed up a large acorn with a half dozen or so spindly twigs for legs. Lucy cried out in horror—the acorn looked like a giant spider—but Oliver didn't seem to notice and just sat back on the floor in a daze. The acorn wobbled for a moment as if its legs might buckle and then began to crawl away. Panicking, Lucy squashed it with the jar of sunstone cream. The spider acorn sizzled and smoked, and then crumbled into ash.

The sunstone cream—it was their only defense now against the Shadow Woods.

"We've been duped, Oliver," Lucy said, smearing the rest of the cream all over herself. "Pop was hired to fix the clock, but not in the way we thought. We've got to save him and get out of here."

"It was Teddy," Oliver said—he was awake, his eyes clear in the red light from the chandelier. "I remember now. He forced me to eat that acorn—it gave me the most horrible nightmare—but I couldn't wake up. And Mom. She was—"

Oliver shuddered, and Lucy tossed aside the empty jar of sunstone cream.

"It's all right now," she said, helping him to his feet. "But I need you to keep it together so we can all get out of here."

"You don't understand. It's Teddy—he's not what he seems!"

"Neither is Mr. Quigley. He's the one who rerouted the pipes into the shadow wood. You were right all along about the clock, Oliver—but Mr. Quigley is working for the Garr!"

"What are you talking about? Where's Pop?"

"The Shadow Woods have him trapped in his bedroom. But the sunstone cream will protect us. We can save Pop—come on!"

Lucy and Oliver raced to their father's bedroom. The

door was still closed, but Lucy could hear him squealing and struggling within. Working together, the children shoved the door open just enough so Lucy could slip her hand inside. Her fingers brushed one of the branches and it immediately recoiled with a *hiss!* The door swung open, and as Lucy and Oliver burst into the room, the branches withdrew to the window, avoiding the children and releasing their father.

Mr. Tinker sprang up from his bed and pushed Lucy and Oliver out into the hallway, slamming the door behind them. "Thank goodness you're safe!" he cried, breathless. "How did you—?"

"We're leaving, Pop," Lucy said. "Just stay between Oliver and me, and we can protect you from the branches. If we make it to the other side of the river, we'll be safe."

"Lucy, what are you talking about?"

"There's no time to explain. We need to get out of here now!"

The Tinkers ran. Oliver grabbed his glasses from their bedroom, Mr. Tinker snatched the truck keys from the kitchen counter, and in the next moment, they were in the foyer heading for the front door.

"The animals," Lucy cried, stopping. "We can't leave the animals!"

"What animals?" asked Mr. Tinker, but Lucy was

already hurrying through the parlor and into the library. The animals were gone—back in their hiding spot, Lucy knew—and she squatted down by the secret door in the bookcase.

"Torsten!" she cried frantically. "Meridian—everyone! We need to get out of here now. The Shadow Woods have reached the house. The Garr will be here any minute." No response. "Please listen! You can come with us. Blackford House is lost, but we can all survive if we leave now! I almost forgot—we can use the secret passageway in the fireplace!"

"Lucy, what are you doing?" her father asked. He and Oliver stood watching from the library door, their eyes huge with fear and confusion. Suddenly, it was all too much for her, and Lucy burst into tears.

"I'm *not* the caretaker!" she cried. "I should've told you both, but I thought I could help the animals. I thought I could save the house and—"

Lucy's father went to her and held her close. "Sweetie, it's all right. But come on, we need to get out of here."

"But the animals," Lucy said, sobbing. "You don't understand—"

"I love you and your brother, that's all I need to understand. And I'm not going to let anything happen to you. Now, come on, before more trees break inside."

Just then, the lights dimmed for a moment and brightened again. Lucy stopped crying.

"The atmospheric changes," Oliver said, looking around. "If the shadow wood absorbs our fear—I remember now what Teddy said! The sunstone absorbs our love. That means there's still a chance—a chance to fix the clock and counteract the shadow wood."

"Ollie, what are you talking about?" cried his father. "We need to get out of here!"

"It's the house," Lucy said, wiping away her tears. "It's talking to us—telling us there's still hope. Hope is the antidote to fear. The Garr hasn't come inside yet, which means maybe the sunstone here is still too strong for him. He needs more fear to destroy what's left."

"Who is the Garr? Will someone please tell me what's going on?"

"I don't know what I was thinking," Lucy said, gazing out the window. She could no longer see the large patch of overgrown grass in the moonlight. The Shadow Woods had grown over it. Lucy shivered. Would they be able to make it through those trees before the sunstone cream wore off? And even if it didn't, one wrong move and they'd be dead. As for the secret passageway, the thought that the Shadow Woods might trap them down there was too much to bear.

All this ran through Lucy's mind in a split-second, but

in the end, the biggest problem was still the Garr.

"The Garr won't let us leave," she said, turning back to the others. "But he still can't come inside. It's our love that's keeping him out—which means there is still enough magic left in the sunstone. Our only hope then is to fix the clock and restore the balance. That will keep the Garr and the Shadow Woods away for good."

Mr. Tinker just gaped at Lucy in confusion.

"I don't understand everything Lucy's talking about either, Pop, but I trust her," Oliver said, pushing up his glasses. "And I *do* know that everything Mr. Quigley and Teddy told us is a lie. It's our fear, *my* fear that got the clock ticking again. I should've put it together when Lucy screamed upstairs and the pendulum moved. Same thing after my first nightmare when I noticed the Shadow Woods had overtaken the carriage house."

"Don't you see, Pop?" Lucy said. "If your love for us can make those lights flicker without any pipes at all connected to the clock face, then there's still hope. That's what the house is trying to tell us!"

"Lucy, I—"

"There's magic here; Pop, you've got to believe me! And there's a monster in the woods who wants that magic for himself. The Garr."

At that moment, the secret door in the bookcase opened,

and the animals poked their heads into the library.

"Your children are telling you the truth, Mr. Tinker," said Meridian.

Mr. Tinker gasped and staggered backward. His knees buckled, and he leaned on the chemistry table for support.

"You—you can—*talk!*" he stammered in disbelief.

"That's what I was trying to tell you, Pop," Lucy said.

"My name is Fennish," said the rat, coming forward. "I've seen many wondrous things here in my time, Mr. Tinker, but never courage as strong as your daughter's. And if your love for your children can make those lights flicker, then Miss Lucy is not the only caretaker here. *All of you* are."

"But—this is—impossible," Mr. Tinker stammered. Oliver, however, calmly stepped toward the animals and smiled.

"I don't know what's going on either, Pop," he said. "But I want to help. I'm tired of being afraid all the time."

Mr. Tinker considered this for a moment and then, with a heavy sigh, said, "I trust you, Lucy. I trust you both. What do you need me to do?"

Lucy threw her arms around his waist and hugged him.

"First we need to stop the pendulum," she said, moving to the door. "I tried, but I wasn't strong enough. Maybe all of us, working together—"

"The pendulum has stopped only once in over a hundred

years," said Meridian. "When the Garr arrived. The burst of evil from the Shadow Woods was so strong it threw off the balance here. And now that the clock is powered by fear, there is no way to stop the pendulum."

"Perpetual motion," Oliver said. "The Shadow Woods are here in the house now. They feed the clock just as the clock feeds them."

"And even if you stopped the clock," said Duck, "the Shadow Woods are already here—*quack-quack!*"

"But we've *got* to stop the clock!" cried Torsten. "If we don't, the house will die! *All* of us will die!"

"Hang on," Lucy said, "if a burst of evil from the Shadow Woods stopped the clock the first time, do you think maybe a burst of *good* could stop it now?"

Mr. Tinker rubbed his forehead. "But, if I follow you, the only way to do that would be to reroute some pipes into the clock face. And that would take days!"

"Not to mention the clock face was originally built for *us*," said Torsten.

"That's it!" said Fennish. "The clock face was built for *us*!"

"What do you mean, old friend?" asked Meridian, but before Fennish could explain, a shadow wood branch crashed in through the library window and went straight for him. Oliver hurled himself in front of it, shielding the rat with his body, and the branch disintegrated into ash as soon as it touched his back.

"Retreat, retreat!" cried Fennish, and in the next moment, Tempus Crow flew in through the broken window and dive-bombed Mr. Tinker.

"He's alive!" Torsten howled. "Tempus Crow is alive!"

Everything next happened at once. Lucy shrieked, and Mr. Tinker, swatting blindly as the crow attacked, backed out of sight into the parlor. Oliver ran after him, and then the animals latched onto Lucy's nightgown and dragged her back into the hiding spot. The secret door in the bookcase closed behind them, and Lucy found herself inside a narrow, darkened shaft with a set of stone stairs curving upward into the shadows behind her. The only source of light was a small crack higher up in the bookcase. Lucy could just make out a set of smaller, animal-size stairs leading up to it in the gloom.

Lucy restrained herself from screaming and sat there with her heart hammering as Nessie hopped up the stairs and peeked out the crack. At the same time, the slam of the front door shook the walls, and a muffled voice shouted:

"That's enough, Tempus!"

"It's the old clocksmith," Nessie whispered, and Lucy heard him cough.

"It's Mr. Quigley!" she whispered in terror, and as if in reply, a low creak echoed through the house. "What's happening to my father, to Oliver?"

The rabbit pressed one of her long ears to the peephole, blocking out the light entirely. "They're all right. But one wrong move, Mr. Quigley says, and he'll shoot."

Lucy gasped. "Mr. Quigley has a gun!" she cried, and Meridian shushed her.

"Now Mr. Quigley's asking where *you* are, Miss Lucy," Nessie said. "Tempus Crow saw us. Oh no, he knows about the hiding spot—they're coming into the library!"

"Quiet, everyone, not a sound!" Meridian hissed. Reginald squealed, Torsten whimpered, and then came the sound of footsteps shuffling into the library.

"Down on the floor, the both of you!" ordered Mr. Quigley. "Where's Lucy?"

"Er—she must have jumped out the window," Mr. Tinker said shakily, and then a loud thump on the other side of the bookcase startled everyone. Lucy slapped her hand over her mouth to keep from screaming.

"In-SIDE—*caw!*" Tempus Crow cried throatily, and Mr. Quigley pounded on the bookcase.

"Open up, you loathsome creatures!" the old man shouted.

Nessie hopped down from the crack—"Out of the way, out of the way!" she whispered—and Mr. Quigley was heard knocking some books off the shelves. Lucy and the animals backed up and around the curve of the stone stairs, and then—*bang!*—a bullet ripped a hole through the bookcase, casting a dot of red light on the stone wall. Lucy and the animals huddled together, their hearts hammering against one another in panic.

"Mr. Quigley, no!" cried Lucy's father from the library. "Let the children go—"

"Another move and you die!" the old man snapped, then he began coughing into his handkerchief. "Curséd soot! What, no more tricks, house? No more candlesticks?"

The walls creaked and groaned.

"I thought as much! You're too weak now, aren't you, house? Very soon, the magic in your sunstone will be depleted, and your light will be gone forever!" Mr. Quigley laughed. "Now, where's the secret switch to open the bookcase, Tinker?"

"We don't know, I swear! We don't even know what's going on!"

"Maybe this will make you talk!"

"No, please, not my son!"

"Alive GOOD—*caw!* Fear help Ed-GAR!"

Lucy gasped—did she hear the bird correctly?

Mr. Quigley sighed. "Perhaps you're right, Tempus," he said calmly, and pounded on the bookcase again. "Go ahead and hide, then! The house is almost ready. Your fear will only help Edgar!"

"Ed-GAR—*caw!*"

Lucy's skin broke out into gooseflesh. She understood. Tempus Crow had not said *"The Garr!"* when he deserted the clock that night three months ago. He'd cried out the name of the Blackfords' long lost son—which meant little Eddie was the Garr!

"Of course," Meridian whispered. "The only one of us Eddie ever liked was Tempus Crow. He would sit there on the landing for hours just to watch him cuckoo. Tempus must have sensed his presence that night in the Shadow Woods and flew off to find him! Little Eddie is the Garr!"

"Impossible—*oink!* Edgar Blackford died over a hundred years ago—*oink-oink!*"

"The Shadow Woods," Fennish said quietly. "They transformed him into even more of a monster than he was before."

"But how?" Torsten said. "And why? After all these years, why would Edgar suddenly come back for his house three months ago?"

"That's when Mr. Quigley said he bought the house," Lucy said, the light dawning. "You don't think—"

"Mr. Quigley, please," said Mr. Tinker. "Surely you can let us go. We only came to fix the clock!"

"Yes, and a pretty penny it cost me, too," said Mr. Quigley. "But then again, turning lead into gold is nothing for me."

"He's an alchemist," Meridian whispered. "You heard him. He can turn lead into gold. Which means he must have come to Watch Hollow for the same reasons the Blackfords did over a century ago. He knows about the magic here!"

"Unfortunately," the old man went on, "I got more than I bargained for when I acquired this house. Who would've thought my activities in the Shadow Woods would've brought a monster back from the dead? But no matter, just like you, Charles Tinker, my debts will soon be paid. Edgar will have his house back, and I shall have what's mine."

"The fool," Meridian said. "He resurrected Edgar Blackford by accident when he tried to use the magic in the Shadow Woods for alchemy!"

"I've heard enough," said Fennish, heading up the stairs. "We need to get up into the clock. I know the way. Follow me."

"But what about Edgar?" asked Frederick. "He'll be here any moment now!"

"That's right," said Fennish, his one eye twinkling in the light from the bullet hole. "And we shall be waiting to welcome him home."

FIFTEEN

A SORT OF HOMECOMING

As Mr. Quigley settled into one of the library's big leather armchairs, the crow perched itself above his shoulder on the seatback. There was something strange yet familiar about the bird's eyes, but Oliver couldn't tell for sure being so far away. He was sitting on the floor in front of the chemistry table, huddling close to his father—their minds barely able to comprehend what was happening, let alone what to do about it.

"So, you see, gentlemen," Mr. Quigley said, leveling the gun at them, "at first, I was able to hide my real motives from the house because it was so preoccupied with the disappearance of Tempus Crow and the clock animals."

"But— You speak of the house as if it's—*alive*."

"Oh, but it is, Mr. Tinker. Not in the natural sense, say, as you and I are alive. But you see, the very nature of life here in Watch Hollow is . . . well, *super*-natural."

Mr. Quigley chuckled, then coughed into his handkerchief. Oliver's head was spinning, but he had a good idea what the rat named Fennish had in mind. However, to accomplish it, Lucy and the animals would need to get into the clock. And how they were going to do that with Mr. Quigley sitting right there in front of the secret door in the bookcase, Oliver had no idea.

"Anyhow," the old man continued, "thanks to a

combination of the missing animals, the fear from those that remained, and, of course, the broken clock, the house grew weaker, and I was able to reroute the pipes without it noticing. However, before I could get the magic flowing from the shadow wood, the rat surprised me and blew my cover." Mr. Quigley coughed and adjusted his bandage. "The house evicted me in its way soon after. I couldn't go back in without risking everything."

"So that's why you hired me," Mr. Tinker said glumly.

"And your *children*," said Mr. Quigley. "It was a foolproof plan, you see. All of you were good, innocent people, and I knew the house would welcome your energy. However— and this is the key, Mr. Tinker—even if your winding mechanism failed, I knew, in time, your children's fear would succeed in getting the clock ticking again. After all, there is no fear more powerful than that of a child. Think back to those nightmares of long ago, Mr. Tinker. Or to those long, dark nights spent huddled under your blankets, cowering from the monster under your bed. Have you ever known such fear?"

"Yes, I have," Mr. Tinker said sadly. "The fear of losing my children."

Mr. Quigley scoffed. "You're too sentimental for your own good, *Charles*," he said, and then the old man's eyes flickered with understanding. "Then again, perhaps that is the problem. Perhaps that is why Edgar has yet to return. There must still be too much hope, too much *love* in the house—which means we need more *fear*!"

Mr. Quigley pointed the gun at Oliver.

"No!" cried his father. Oliver cowered against the leg of the chemistry table, and then—*bang!*—one of the beakers exploded above their heads. Mr. Quigley howled with laughter—he had missed Oliver on purpose. At the same time, more Shadow Wood branches slithered in through the broken window and fanned out like fingers over one of the bookcases. The burst of fear from Oliver and his father had brought the trees closer!

"There, you see?" said Mr. Quigley. "Perpetual motion. Fear begets fear, just as love begets love. However, fear is much stronger than love. Think of the power, then, in that precise moment when a son realizes he is about to lose his father."

The old man turned the gun on Mr. Tinker. Oliver screamed, the Shadow Woods crept farther into the room, and then a booming voice bellowed from outside:

"BRING ME THE TINKERS!"

Oliver nearly fainted with fright. It was the Garr!

"Ed-*GAR!*" cried Tempus Crow, flying out of the room, and Mr. Quigley smiled.

"You heard him," the old man said, rising. "Hands up

and outside. However, I warn you: one false move, Charles, and your son gets it."

Mr. Quigley led Oliver and his father at gunpoint out onto the porch, where a red-eyed, ten-foot-tall tree man stood waiting for them in the moonlight at the bottom of the steps. Oliver's knees buckled, and his father pulled him closer, the two of them shaking as the monster leaned in to get a closer look at them.

"*WHERE IS THE GIRL?*" the Garr growled, his breath rotten and steaming from his glowing red mouth.

"She's inside somewhere, hiding with the animals," said Mr. Quigley. "You needn't worry about them now. The clock is ticking and the house is ready. Therefore, allow me to be the first one to welcome you home, Master Blackford!"

Mr. Quigley chuckled, and so did the Garr—low and croaking, like a frog—and then his glowing red eyes and mouth melted together, his tree body shrank to the shape and size of a human, and there in the moonlight stood the same boy Oliver had seen standing at the edge of the Shadow Woods. Teddy, aka Edgar Blackford!

"I owe you Tinkers much gratitude," he said, mounting the steps to the porch. "The fear you have helped create here tonight has enabled me to come home."

Mr. Quigley pulled the Tinkers aside, and as Edgar walked past them into the house, Oliver caught a whiff of the same garbagy odor he had smelled so many times near the tunnel in the Shadow Woods.

Mr. Quigley led Oliver and his father back inside at gunpoint. Edgar was standing at the foot of the stairs now, gazing up at the clock with the crow perched on the banister beside him.

"All right, you have your house back," said Mr. Quigley. "I kept my end of the bargain. Now kindly return my book of formulas and I'll be on my way."

So that was how Edgar Blackford got Mr. Quigley to do his dirty work, Oliver realized amid his terror. He had taken the old man's book of formulas!

Edgar giggled and turned around to face him. "You old fool. Did you really think I would allow you to leave here with the knowledge of the Shadow Woods?"

"But we made a deal!" cried Mr. Quigley. "This house is rightfully mine! I agreed to give it to you in exchange for my book of formulas, which you stole from me when I was practicing my art in the Shadow Woods!"

Edgar swiveled his gaze to Oliver. "This is what happens when a bumbling alchemist comes to Watch Hollow seeking immortality. My parents settled here for the same reasons. However, unlike Mr. Quigley, they were talented. They failed to make themselves immortal, of course, but they did succeed in other magical pursuits—such as carving wooden animals that come alive and, of course, building this house and its clock."

"Where is my book?" Mr. Quigley persisted, but Edgar just ignored him and looked up again at the clock.

"I suppose Mr. Quigley learned of Watch Hollow the way most alchemists learn of such places—through research, astronomical calculations, and whatnot. Luckily for him, the house had come into the possession of a distant relation of mine in England who was unaware of its . . . *uniqueness*. Mr. Quigley acquired it for a song, I'm sure."

"My *book!*" the old man cried. Oliver could feel him trembling with rage behind him. If only he could use this wrinkle in things to his advantage and distract everyone so Lucy and the animals could get up into the clock. *Think, Oliver, think!*

"Alas," Edgar said, turning back with a sigh. "Poor Mortimer Quigley. In his quest for immortality, he made *me* come alive instead—and much more powerful than I could have ever dreamed as a boy. I am one now with the Shadow Woods, my magic as ancient and mysterious as the trees themselves. And finally, after all these years, I'm able to come home."

Edgar giggled, and Mr. Quigley stepped out from behind the Tinkers.

"Enough!" the old man said, pointing his gun now at

Edgar. "This is your last chance. Give me my book of formulas or I will send you back into the darkness where you belong."

"Your book is destroyed," Edgar said, smiling mischievously. "After all, you won't be needing it where you're going."

Mr. Quigley wailed in frustration and fired—*bang, bang!*—hitting Edgar square in the chest. Oliver and his father jumped back, while Edgar just glanced down casually at the bullet holes in his shirt and giggled.

"Ouch," he said, and then in a burst of red sparkles, the holes closed as if they were never there. Mr. Quigley's eyes bulged in horror; but before he could fire again, Edgar waved his hand, and a giant shadow wood branch exploded out of the library. It barreled through the parlor like a freight train, knocking furniture everywhere and snatching Mr. Quigley off his feet. Oliver's father pulled him close, the two of them trembling as the branch shook Mr. Quigley so hard he dropped his gun—along with dozens of gold coins from his pockets.

"Help, help!" the old man shrieked, and then the branch dragged him backward, kicking and screaming, through the parlor and out the library window into the Shadow Woods. Mr. Quigley's screams choked off a second later.

"My parents never trusted me with *their* book of formulas either," Edgar said, smiling. "But who needs alchemy when one wields the power of the Shadow Woods? Take Tempus Crow." Edgar stroked the giant bird's head. "All he needed was a pair of new acorns in his eyes after Lucy nearly killed him—the same acorns that gave you your nightmares, Oliver Tinker."

Despite his fear, Oliver understood. He'd noticed the crow's eyes in the library—that was it; they were made of acorns! Tempus Crow had been the clock's cuckoo bird, which meant his eyes had once been made of sunstones. That's how Edgar Blackford was controlling him. He'd replaced the bird's eyes with acorns!

"And yet," Edgar went on, "looking back, I suppose I've always known that I was destined to wield the power of the Shadow Woods—which is why, all those years ago, I tried replacing Fennish's eyes with acorns, too. Unfor tunately, however, my parents intervened and—" Edgar looked around. "Well, speaking of Fennish, where is our lucky number seven? I am so looking forward to killing him."

At that moment, something clanged in the mechanical room. Edgar turned toward the clock, and Tempus Crow flew up to the cuckoo door and tried to pry it open with his beak. Lucy and the animals had made it up there after all, Oliver realized—and at the same time, his father leaned over and whispered in his ear.

"I know what they're doing," he said. "You need to get up there and help!"

"What do you mean?"

"In-SIDE—*caw!*" cried Tempus Crow, struggling with the cuckoo door; and as Edgar stepped onto the stairs, Mr. Tinker rushed across the foyer and tackled him from behind. Edgar cried out in surprise, and then the two of them tumbled together onto the floor.

"NOW, OLIVER, GO!" cried his father.

Oliver shook off his stupor, his fear, his worry, and with single-minded purpose bounded up the stairs and into the mechanical room, where he found the others stretched out in a human-animal chain between the clock face and the conductor sphere. Fennish held onto the sphere with his front paws, Meridian held onto his back legs, Torsten hung on to her tail, then came the pig, the rabbit, the turtle, the duck, the squirrel, the beaver, the skunk, the fawn, and the raccoon, whose tail was wrapped around Lucy's ankle. Lucy was balancing on one foot, reaching like a ballet dancer with her fingers only inches from the clock face.

But still, their human-animal chain was too short!

"Oliver, help!" Lucy cried, her face contorted with strain—but before Oliver could make a move, Tempus Crow flew into the mechanical room and dove straight for him. Oliver ducked and swatted blindly at the bird, and then Fennish leaped from the conductor sphere and knocked Tempus Crow to the floor. Jaws snapped and claws slashed, Tempus Crow shrieked, and then the rat and the bird wrestled out of sight behind some gears at the rear of the clock.

"Oliver, now!" Lucy cried. The animals had shifted, and Lucy's hand was on the clock face. Oliver stepped into Fennish's place, and Meridian immediately wrapped her paws around his ankle. At the same time, Edgar Blackford appeared in the doorway.

"NO!" he roared, his eyes blazing with fury, and Oliver teetered over on one leg and slapped his hands down on the conductor sphere.

All at once, a low humming began, and every cell in Oliver's body buzzed. The light in the mechanical room turned from red to blinding white, and then Edgar Blackford screamed and doubled over, clutching his stomach. He staggered backward out onto the landing, the railing split with a deafening *crack*, and then came the muffled thud of Edgar's body on the foyer floor below.

"It's w-w-working!" Lucy shouted, voice shaky and body trembling. "The sunstone is w-w-working!"

"I-c-c-can't hold-d-d on," Torsten cried. "The c-c-current is too strong!"

Oliver gazed down at the little dog. His face was twisted

in agony, as were the faces of the other animals, and in the next moment, the chain broke apart and the animals collapsed to the floor. The mechanical room was engulfed in darkness, but Oliver's eyes were full of floaters. He braced himself on the conductor sphere. His legs felt weak; and his ears, his tongue, his entire body was still buzzing.

And yet, the clock was eerily quiet.

"The pendulum!" Lucy cried. "It's stopped!"

The animals cheered, and then Oliver's only thought was of his father.

Oliver staggered out onto the landing. The railing was smashed, the foyer was dark, and as his floaters dissolved, Oliver caught sight of Edgar Blackford crawling for the open door in a shaft of moonlight. Gold coins were scattered everywhere, and Mr. Tinker sat slumped over at the bottom of the stairs.

Oliver cried out and flew down to him, dropping to his knees and cradling his father in his arms.

"Please don't die, Pop!" Oliver whimpered, the tears beginning to flow. His father was bleeding from the side of his head. Oliver shook him and then, out of the corner of his eye, spied Edgar Blackford rising to his feet within the moonlit doorway. His eyes flashed and began to glow red.

"That's it, yes," Edgar moaned, stepping closer, and through Oliver's tears, he could see that Edgar was turning into the tree man again. "Give me your fear—the delicious fear of losing someone you love!"

Edgar's arms, which had become branches, began extending toward Mr. Tinker. Oliver cried out and shielded him with his body as Edgar's twig-like fingers uncurled only inches away—when out of nowhere, Tempus Crow swooped down from the landing and latched onto Edgar's face.

"My EYES—*caw!*" he cried, wings beating and claws scratching. "Tricked ME—*caw-caw!*"

Oliver caught a fleeting glimpse of the bird's eyes, which looked black and empty in the moonlight, but then Edgar roared and swatted Tempus Crow away, sending him careening through the air and into the darkened dining room, where he slammed into something with a terrible *crash!*

Edgar howled with rage, shaking the walls and rattling the gold coins at his feet, then swelled to twice his size.

"NOW ALL OF YOU SHALL DIE!" he bellowed—when suddenly, Lucy leaped off the landing and onto Edgar Blackford's back.

"Get out of our house!" she cried. Yellow sparkles exploded everywhere, Edgar wailed in pain and began to shrink, and in the next moment, the two of them whirled together out onto the porch.

Oliver shrieked and dashed outside after them.

Edgar was stumbling down the steps now, screaming and flailing his tree arms awkwardly as Lucy rode him piggyback. Plumes of smoke billowed out from them and mixed with the sparkles, and the air grew thick with the smell of garbage and burning wood. Lucy choked and coughed but held on, and all at once Oliver understood.

The sunstone. If Edgar Blackford was one with the Shadow Woods, then the sunstone magic still present in the children's bodies—from both the cream and the clock—was just as deadly to him as it was to the branches in the house!

Oliver flew at Edgar, threw his arms around his waist, and, in an explosion of smoke and sparkles, the three of them fell together in the driveway—Oliver holding Edgar from the front, Lucy holding him from the back.

Edgar screamed in agony and began pummeling Oliver's head, but the blows were weak. Oliver held his breath and squeezed tighter as Edgar's screams turned to moans. The blows tapered off, and then all at once, Oliver felt the monster dissolve into a pile of ashes beneath him.

Oliver hitched in his breath, and as the children rolled over onto their bottoms, the sparkles evaporated all around them. An icy blast of wind whipped across the yard, sweeping the ashes into the darkness, and then the world was silent.

"The Shadow Woods," Lucy said, pointing at the house. "They've backed away— *look!*"

Oliver rose unsteadily to his feet. The Shadow Woods *had* retreated somewhat—he could see the patch of long grass now on the library side of the house—but he was too worried about their father to care.

"We've got to help Pop," he said, choking back sobs. "Edgar hurt him bad."

"There might be a way if you hurry," Meridian called, and the children turned to find the clock animals watching them from the porch. Torsten was the closest—he stood about halfway down the steps.

And between his teeth was a large leather book.

SIXTEEN

GOODBYE & GOOD MORNING

"Don't strain yourself, Pop," Lucy said, holding the lantern closer, and her father smiled down at her from atop the ladder.

"Never felt better, kid," he said with a wink, and then finished ratcheting the last of the clock's pipe couplings. "That should do it."

Oliver and the animals moved aside out onto the landing, their shadows shifting and swelling on the walls as Lucy helped her father drag the ladder out from the mechanical room. Sunrise was almost upon them, and everyone had been working feverishly to get to this moment.

Thanks to Torsten, the children had found a formula for an elixir in Roger Blackford's journal that healed their father almost instantly. And while Lucy tended to him in the library, Oliver and the animals set about dismantling the pipes from the shadow wood and reconnecting the old ones to the clock face.

Luckily, Mr. Quigley had stored the original pipes in the cellar—the door to which magically opened while Lucy and Meridian were searching the pantry for ingredients for the elixir. It was the house speaking to them again, they understood—the damage done by Edgar Blackford and the Shadow Woods still threatened to destroy its magic forever. They needed to repair the clock before it was too late!

"Let's get moving," Oliver said, checking his watch. "It's almost dawn."

With the pipes now in place, the only thing left was to get the animals back into their holes before sunrise so they could fit themselves perfectly inside. Oliver had theorized that, once the balance of magnetic—er, *magical*—energies was restored, all that it would take to get the clock ticking again was a simple push on the pendulum. That was the plan anyway, and everyone understood that it was now or never.

"Let's GO—*caw!*" cried Tempus Crow, fluttering up through the cuckoo door, and Lucy gazed down fondly at Fennish. If not for him, they would've never gotten their cuckoo bird back.

Lucy had seen the whole thing just seconds before the pendulum stopped and the mechanical room was engulfed in darkness. Fennish quickly got the better of Tempus during their fight and, with a single swipe of his paw, knocked out the big bird's acorn eyes. Tempus then flew out of the clock and blindly attacked Edgar, distracting him long enough for Lucy to jump on him from behind. Fortunately, Tempus had only been knocked unconscious; and after a sip of the magical elixir and a new pair of sunstone eyes (Lucy found them in a jar in the library) the old crow was as good as new.

"Does this mean we're alchemists now, Pop?" Lucy

asked as the animals gathered around the ladder, and her father chuckled.

"What gave you that idea?"

"Well, you know, because we used magical formulas and stuff to cure you and Tempus."

"Alchemy is not just about formulas and magic," Meridian said. "It's about transformation—about making things better. The moment you Tinkers arrived here you began to make things better. So, I suppose one could say you've been alchemists all along."

"Well, then you animals are alchemists, too," Lucy said. "We couldn't have saved Blackford House without you."

"Forgive the pun," Fennish said, "but we're not out of the woods yet. You heard the lad, it's almost dawn."

The animals tittered excitedly, and the Tinkers began assisting them back into their holes. Lucy gently inserted Frederick into his *five*, while Oliver climbed up the ladder and placed the fawn (whose name was Dorothy) into the *eleven*. Then he helped Duck into her *two* and Gretchen the skunk into her *one*. Samson the squirrel scurried up the big hand into his *ten*, while Erwin the raccoon pulled himself up onto the little hand and slipped into his *four*. Nessie hopped up the ladder and jumped into her *three*, Mr. Tinker placed Cecily the beaver on the opposite side in her *nine*, and then Oliver climbed down the ladder and helped Lucy lift Reginald into his *eight*. That left only Meridian, Fennish, and Torsten, who sat watching from the stairs leading up to the second floor.

"All right, guys," Lucy said, gesturing for them to get into their holes, but instead, Torsten threw his paws around Lucy's leg and hugged her.

"Thank you for everything, Miss Lucy," he said. "Don't forget to stop by now and then, will you? You know, just to say hello."

"Well, it's not goodbye just yet," Lucy said. "We're still staying for the summer. And hopefully—" Lucy met her father's eyes. With everything that had happened, she hadn't had time to ask him about maybe living in Watch Hollow *for good*. "Well, what with Mr. Quigley being gone now, who's going to be the caretaker?"

"Lucy's right, Pop," Oliver said. "We can't just leave now, can we?"

"Whoa, whoa, one thing at a time," said Mr. Tinker, chuckling. "Let's get the clock ticking again, and we can figure out all that other stuff later, okay?"

Lucy and Oliver exchanged a knowing smile—they could tell just by their father's reaction that he was thinking about staying here for good, too.

"You see?" Lucy said, turning back to Torsten. "Either way, it's not goodbye."

"You don't understand," Meridian said, coming closer. "Once we're back in the clock and it starts ticking, we will turn wooden again forever."

Lucy gasped, and her heart began to beat very fast. "No!" she cried, scooping up Torsten into her arms. "Then I won't let you!"

"And I won't either," said Mr. Tinker. "There must be some other way."

"We were never meant to be alive, Mr. Tinker," Fennish said. "Not like this. That was an accident, born out of Edgar Blackford's return and a blast of evil from the Shadow Woods. We are as much to blame for the balance being lost here as he was."

"That's not *true*," Oliver said, his voice cracking. "And even if it were, what difference does it make? You're alive now, and that's all that matters."

"Please," said Mr. Tinker. "There's no need to sacrifice your lives. Let me try to figure out a way to get the clock ticking again without you."

"There's no time," Torsten said. "And without us, Blackford House will die and its magic will be lost forever."

"And we cannot let that happen," said Fennish. "We clock animals bring the balance here; and in that balance, there is something greater—powerful magic that can transform the world far beyond the reaches of Watch Hollow. It is up to you then, Tinker family, to use that magic wisely."

Fennish hopped up into his *seven* hole, and Lucy's head began to spin. She knew deep down that what the animals were saying was true. She could somehow feel that the house had gotten even weaker— not to mention that nothing magical, not even a groan from the walls, had occurred since the cellar door opened. But was that such a bad thing? After all, what good was a magical house if the price for living in it was losing the ones you loved?

"You Tinkers are the caretakers," Meridian said. "It is up to you to make sure the magic here is used for good. That is what the caretaker does."

Lucy moaned. "But if you go back into the clock, you'll die!"

"Nothing ever really dies," Fennish said. "There is only transformation into something greater. Besides"—he pointed to his head—"we will always be alive in here."

"And in *here*," Torsten said, touching Lucy's heart.

"Come now, it is time," Fennish said. Meridian rubbed her body against Lucy's leg, and for the first time ever, the cat began to purr. Then she bounded up the ladder and leaped into her *twelve* hole. Lucy hugged Torsten tight.

"I love you," she said. "All of you—I love you."

"And we love you," Torsten said. "And therein lies the greatest magic of all."

Torsten smiled and licked Lucy's cheek, and then the little dog jumped from her arms and squeezed into his *six* hole.

"Goodbye!" the clock animals cried. They adjusted their positions to fit their holes and, in the blink of an eye, turned wooden again.

Lucy's heart squeezed and she dragged her wrist across her nose.

"It's not fair," she said, sniffling, and her father held her close.

"Go ahead, Ollie," he said, and Oliver reluctantly stepped into the mechanical room and gave the pendulum a push. It moved effortlessly. Springs boinged and gears clanked, the pendulum started swinging with a slow but steady *tick—tock—tick—tock*, and as the hands spun around to the proper time, lights all over the house flickered to life in halos of luminescent white.

Lucy heaved a heavy sigh. The clock was fixed, but she felt sadder than ever.

"Well, I suppose, that's it then," Mr. Tinker said blandly, and then something entirely unexpected happened there on the landing: the railing through which Edgar Blackford had fallen began repairing itself! Pieces of wood, big and small, flew up from the foyer and joined together, cracks sealed all by themselves, and soon, every splinter was back in place and the railing looked as good as new.

"But that's—" Mr. Tinker stopped himself from saying *impossible*. He knew better by now—*nothing*, it seemed, was impossible here in Watch Hollow.

"It's the love from the animals," Oliver said, gazing around in wonder. "It's more powerful than ever."

Lucy watched in disbelief as the color oozed back into the wallpaper, the shadow wood began to shine as if freshly polished, and the sound of tinkling glass came from—

"My windows!" Lucy exclaimed.

The Tinkers hurried downstairs and arrived at the library just in time to see the shattered panes flying back into place as if they had never been shattered at all. Lucy's heart soared. The sky was dull gray with the first light of dawn, but her windows seemed to gleam more brilliantly than ever.

"Look!" Oliver cried, pointing outside, and Lucy gasped. The Shadow Woods were dissolving backward into the gloom!

The Tinkers raced through the house and out onto the porch. Lucy could hardly believe her eyes. Where the Shadow Woods once stood at the end of the driveway, rolling lawns and flowering trees stretched out against a yellow-orange horizon. In the distance to her left, Lucy could make out part of the stone bridge and a smudge of the river, and to her right, about fifty yards away, a wide, fence-lined pasture.

The Tinkers hurried down to the bottom of the steps and turned back toward the house. The outside had repaired itself, too. The shingles looked brand-new and the shutters were back in place, flowers blossomed everywhere among the shrubbery, and the grass was freshly mown. The air was thick with the smell of it, along with the sweet fragrance of the violets and daffodils that bloomed along the flagstone paths.

And yet the Shadow Woods were not entirely gone, Lucy realized in the dim morning light—the trees had stopped dissolving behind the house, far off in the distance to her right. But that was okay. The Shadow Woods weren't all bad. They were simply part of the balance here, an essential element to the magic in Watch Hollow—more of a mystery than anything, Lucy had come to realize. And as with any other mystery, one needed to tread carefully.

"You all right, Pop?" Oliver asked, and Mr. Tinker knuckled away a tear.

"I just wish your mother could see this," he said, his voice tight with emotion.

"She can, Pop," Lucy said, with an arm around his waist. "She can."

The Tinkers just stood there for a long time, watching in silence as the world around them brightened—when from out of nowhere, the most beautiful white horse Lucy had ever seen pranced into the pasture. Everyone gasped.

"Come on, let's go see!" Oliver said. But as her father and brother took off across the lawn, Lucy's heart began to hammer. She had seen that horse before.

Lucy bounded back inside the house and into the dining room, where she gazed up at the painting over the buffet. The white horse in the painted pasture was the same as the white horse in the real pasture outside. But there was something else now, too—something Lucy never would have expected in a million years.

The faint outlines of the ghostlike figures had filled in, and there on the steps stood the perfect likenesses of Lucy and her family—only everyone was dressed in old-fashioned clothes, and they were waving to a man in the carriage.

Yes, the outline of *that* figure had filled in, too. The man was young and handsome, and wore a black coat and top hat.

Lucy's skin prickled with excitement—or was it fear? She had no idea who the man was.

But just the same, Lucy Tinker knew that he was coming.

ACKNOWLEDGMENTS

This book is the result of two false starts, three completely different drafts, and the hard work of lots of people besides me. First and foremost, I am eternally indebted to the brilliant Abby Ranger, who came up with the original idea for this story and trusted me to write it. Words simply cannot express how grateful I am to her for this opportunity. Next, boundless thanks to my superb and just all-around-awesome editor, David Linker, for his insight and guidance during the latter half of this process. My sincerest thanks also to Kate Jackson for her patience and understanding, Rose Pleuler for her work on the first draft; Carolina Ortiz, Jon Howard, and Andrea Curley for their work on this one; and to everyone else at HarperCollins involved with this project—thank you, thank you, thank you!

Cheers, as always, to my dear agent, Bill Contardi, without whom I'd be lost. Much love and gratitude to my parents, Anthony and Linda, for their unwavering support during the hardest of times, and to my sitters, Anna Higginson, Kiara Hines, Grace Hamashima, and Lisette Glodowski, for keeping my daughter occupied during those hours when deadlines loomed and I needed to write. Thanks once again to Michael Combs for his friendship and never-ending encouragement, and to the following kind souls for listening when they could have been doing much better things: Carey Blackburn, Jessica Braun, Michael Eubanks, Daniel Fetter, Nicholas Lease, Joseph Lisi, Caroline May, Aubrey Moya-Mendez, Matthew Reda, Darian Rutter, Jane Simmons, Donald Sutton, Pierce Williams, Andrew Antoci, Matt Donahue, Morgan Goodman, Catie Griffin, Jayme Johns, Olivia Manlove, De'Ja McKnabb, Tyler Smith, Kelly Toland, Grant Vandervoort, Joseph Webster, Madeline Whallen, Collin Yates, and Kennedy Young.

And finally, to my dear friend and mentor, the late John Shearin: thank you for continuing to watch over me.

DATE			

9|19   1   4|19

12|21   1   4|19

4|24   1   4|19